BECOMING
HOLMES

THE BOY SHERLOCK HOLMES HIS FINAL CASE

SHANE PEACOCK

Tundra Books

Published in Canada by Tundra Books, a division of Random House of Canada Limited,
One Toronto Street, Suite 300, Toronto, Ontario M5C 2V6

Published in the United States by Tundra Books of Northern New York,
P.O. Box 1030, Plattsburgh, New York 12901

Library of Congress Control Number: 2011938781

Library and Archives Canada Cataloguing in Publication

Peacock, Shane
Becoming Holmes : the boy Sherlock Holmes, his final case / by Shane Peacock.

(The boy Sherlock Holmes ; 6)
ISBN 978-1-77049-232-5. – ISBN 978-1-77049-291-2 (EPUB)

1. Holmes, Sherlock (Fictitious character) – Juvenile fiction.
I. Title. II. Series: Peacock, Shane. Boy Sherlock Holmes ; 6.

PS8581.E234M38 2012 jC813'.54 C2011-906509-6

We acknowledge the financial support of the Government of Canada through the Canada Book Fund and that of the Government of Ontario through the Ontario Media Development Corporation's Ontario Book Initiative. We further acknowledge the support of the Canada Council for the Arts and the Ontario Arts Council for our publishing program.

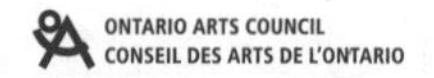

The author wishes to thank Patrick Mannix and Motco Enterprises Ltd., U.K., ref: www.moto.com, for the use of their Edward Stanford's Library Map of London and its suburbs, 1862.

Design by Jennifer Lum

www.tundrabooks.com

Printed and bound in Canada

This book is printed on acid-free paper that is 100% recycled, ancient-forest friendly (100% post-consumer recycled).

1 2 3 4 5 6 17 16 15 14 13 12

To Johanna,
artist and sweetheart.

ACKNOWLEDGMENTS

As The Boy Sherlock Holmes series comes to an end, there are many people to thank. Tundra Books has been a wonderful home for me and my work. Kathy Lowinger was the visionary at first, bringing her bravery and brilliance to bear, allowing these novels to take flight. Catherine Mitchell then sent them sailing off to other countries. Others at Tundra have contributed throughout – Alison Morgan, Pamela Osti, Sylvia Chan, and Jennifer Lum, among the key players. But no one was more important, certainly for me, than Kathryn Cole, one of Canada's premier editors. She piloted me through the first five books with a Sherlock-like wisdom and was missed on this sixth and last. I was lucky, however, to have been partnered with Tara Walker on *Becoming Holmes*. Stepping into big editorial shoes with verve, compassion, and great skill, she helped me steer the Sherlock ship home. I was fortunate to have her as my guide.

Derek Mah was a key ally all the way through this series, his lovely paintings gracing each and every novel, an artist with a sort of Watson-like ability to make his remarkable work much more than just complementary. I would be remiss if I did not mention one Samuel Peacock, whose snake research for this novel was thorough and much appreciated. And I'd also like to thank my agent, Pamela Paul, for all her efforts from day one. Jennifer Stokes's copyediting and Margaret Allen's proofreading were invaluable as well.

My mother, Susan Peacock, who, as I said in my first dedication in this series, "gave me a writer's soul," passed away between the fifth and sixth novels. But she was with me, nevertheless, and will stay in my heart as long as I write and beyond.

And finally, thanks goes to that group of strange people who live with me and deal, together, with the storms of life: Sophie, Johanna, Hadley, and Sam. No one has a better team. We, like the boy Sherlock Holmes, are just beginning.

CONTENTS

CHEAPSIDE
ST. PAULS CHURCH YARD
CANNON STREET WEST
CANNON STR.
POULTRY
BANK OF ENGLAND
ROYAL EXCHANGE
STOCK EXCHANGE
LOMBARD
KING WILLIAM STR.
PRINCES ST.
MANSION HOUSE
GROCERS HALL
MERCERS HALL
DOCTORS COMMONS
ST. MARY LE BOW
ST. AUGUSTINE
ST. MATTHEW
CORDWAINERS HALL
ALL HALLOWS
ST. ANTHOLIN
ST. SWITHIN
ST. CLEMENT
ST. MICHAEL
ST. JAMES
Paternoster Row
Old Fish St.
Pancras L.
Bucklersbury
Abchurch La.
Queen St.
St. Pauls Pier
QUEENHITHE DOCK
Anchor Wh.
Castle Baynard Dock
Honduras Wh.
Willow Wharf
Royal George Wh.
Mason's Stairs
Devonshire Wh.
Globe Wh.
Stone Wh.
Brooks Wharf
Maidstone Wh.
Kennet Wh.
Scots's Wharf
Cast Iron Wharf
SOUTHWARK BRIDGE
Iron Wharf
Carey's Wharf
Dowgate Dock Stairs
Brewery
Steel Yard Wh.
Allhallows Pier
Wellington Wh.
Winchester Wh.
Flour Mill
Phœnix Wharf
St. Mary Overy's Dock
West Kent Wh.
Old Swan Pier Stairs Wharf
LONDON BRIDGE
Fresh Wharf
Cox's Quay
Chamberlain's Wharf
Hibernia Wh.
Love Lane
PHŒNIX GAS WORKS
HOPTONS ALMS HO.
Park Street
Barclay & Perkins' Brewery
Potts' Vinegar Works
Great Guildford
Sumner St.
Essex
York Pl.
BRIDGE STREET
BOROUGH MARKET
ST. SAVIOUR
ST. OLAVES
Duke St.
ST. THOMAS HOSPITAL
GUY'S HOSPITAL
St. Thomas St.
WELLINGTON ST.
CHARING CROSS RAILWAY
Union Street
ST. SAVIOURS PAROCHL. SCHOOL
BOROUGH HIGH STR.
ST. GEORGES WORK HO.
ZION CHAPEL
ST. GEORGE
WHITE STREET
BAPTIST CHAP.
Suffolk Street
Red Cross Co.
Mint St.
Weston Yd.

ALDGATE HIGH ST.
GOODMAN'S FIELDS
LEADENHALL ST.
CROSBY HALL
SYNAGOGUE
PENINSULAR & ORIENTAL STM NAVIGATN CO.
SUSSEX HALL
IRONMONGERS HALL
INDIA DOCK CO'S WAREHOUSES
JEWS ORPHN ASYLUM
GARRICK THEATRE
TRINITY
Gr. Prescot St.
WHITECHAPEL COUNTY COURT
RAILWAY STATION
John St.
Gould Sq.
Chamber Str.
Modiford Co.
ST. MARGARET
Dunster Co.
Commercial Sale Rooms
E. & W. INDIA DOCK COMPANY WARE-HOUSES
CORN EXCHANGE
POLICE STAT.
TRINITY SQUARE
Royal Mint Street
ROYAL MINT
LITTLE TOWER HILL
GREAT TOWER HILL
THAMES STREET
CUSTOM HOUSE
Quay
Ditch
Chapel
White Tower
Armoury
Bridge
THE TOWER
Tower Wharf
Upper East Smithfield
ST KATHARINE DOCKS
(West)
(East)
Basin
Burr St.
Hoare & Co's Red Lion Brewery
Hayes's Wharf
Hayes's Dock
Battle Br. Stairs
Wilson's Wh.
Custom Ho. Stairs (East)
Gun & Shot Wh.
Wool Quay
Galley Dock
Symons Wh.
Stantons Wh.
Phoenix Wh.
Pickle Herring Stairs
Chesters Quay
Brewers Quay
Tower Dock Stairs
Queen's Stairs
Freemans Wh.
Browns Wh.
Goulding's Wh.
Davis' Wh.
Irongate Stairs
Horselydown Stairs
Harrisons Wh.
Butlers Wh.
Georges Stairs
Sufferance Wh.
New Stairs
Millers Wharf
Downe's Wharf
Hermitage
Mill Stairs
UPP
Pickle Herring St.
QUEEN ELIZABETH FREE GRAMMAR SCHOOL
ST JOHNS CHARITY SCHOOL
HORSELYDOWN
ST JOHNS
Queen Elizabeth St.
Artillery
Charles St.
Thornton St.
ST SAVIOUR DOCK
POLICE STATION
Distillery
SCHOOL
London Street
DOCK HEAD
Fashion S.
BERMONDSEY
Market S.
Russell

PREFACE

The streets of Hounslow had seldom seen his like. Descending from his gleaming carriage, he walked silently beneath the gaslights, in and out of darkness, top hat pulled down, his cape shrouding his form, and his walking stick never touching the ground. He eyed the row houses until he stopped at one. He looked in both directions, turned onto the walkway and floated to the door. A gentle knock – three short and three long – let him in. The entrance closed and the neighborhood returned to normal. But this was a different night from any other, for not far down the street, a shadow had observed him.

Another shadow lay in its dark nest south of the River Thames that night, a waste of a man. Crows called outside his marble walls, rats ran through his rooms, and spiders, left to their ways, spun webs the size and thickness of blankets above him. He was naked and sweating, spread upon his filthy stone bed. There were tears in his eyes, tears of joy. A hissing and rustling surrounded him. He had loosed his giant pets, the squeezers and the poisoners. They caressed his legs, his hips, his chest, his big, throbbing head. Though his slithering killers were the world's most deadly, none were as lethal as his thoughts.

"Command me!" he cried to no one.

"Who could come to-night? Some friend of yours, perhaps?"
"Except yourself I have none," he answered. "I do not encourage visitors."

– Dr. Watson and Sherlock Holmes in *The Five Orange Pips*

"I am no doubt indirectly responsible for Dr. Grimesby Roylott's death, and I cannot say that it is likely to weigh very heavily upon my conscience."

– Sherlock Holmes in *The Adventure of the Speckled Band*

1

DEATH

London might as well be draped in black on this thirteenth morning of June in 1870. It is as if every pedestrian imagines dark ribbons hanging upon the buildings across the great city from Westminster to Whitechapel and all along little Denmark Street to the apothecary shop where Sherlock Holmes, sixteen years old and as moody as a young stallion, slumps over the laboratory table, unable to work. A single gaslight is lit in the dim room.

"DICKENS IS DEAD!" read the headlines on the shop's newspapers, now three days old and yet still lying nearby. The funeral will be tomorrow at Westminster Abbey.

But much more than the sudden and shocking death of the age's greatest novelist, the soul of England, haunts young Holmes today. He is deep in one of his black periods. They have descended upon him in short stretches since birth and grown more frequent since his mother's death (which he believes he caused). But he has always thrown them off. When his prodigious brain has been excited by a truly challenging problem or, better still, by the scent of the solution to a crime that no one else can solve, he has always risen to heights of almost erotic energy, like an opium addict with the juice of the poppy plant freshly rushing into his veins.

But the blackness has been with him for too long this time. He cannot shake it. Death and disappointment are all around him, and they are not going away. He is desperate to climb up from the depths. He needs a thrill. He thinks of the dangerous crimes he has solved, recalls the heart-pumping sensation of being near murder, and wonders, for a fleeting second, if he, Sherlock Holmes, about to become a man, should kill someone, someone evil.

He lifts his head slightly and looks at the alkaloids and poisons in his master's cabinets: strychnine, cocaine, tubocurarine, nicotine, morphine, and more. *They do so much for our patients! Would they help me too?*

It is four o'clock in the morning.

To the east in London, at this very hour, a boy of about eighteen, plump, with a narrow brush mustache above his thin lips and blonde hair that is parted too close to the middle and falls limply over his forehead, walks across London Bridge carrying a bag that seems to be breathing. It pulses beneath his grip.

"Settle, pretty things," he says in a high-pitched whine.

There is human blood on his hands. But he won't wash it off, not for hours. He has looked into the face of death again and been fascinated. He is thinking about that, adrenaline still coursing through him.

"Give me more to do, boss, more to do; give me Sherlock Holmes."

A graveyard awaits him.

Back in the dim apothecary shop, Sherlock is startled by another high-pitched but much more friendly voice. "My boy!" cries Sigerson Bell. The old apothecary, bent in the shape of a question mark, comes sliding down the railing of his spiral staircase upon his bum like a child, wearing his nightgown. His long, thin, white hair sails out from under his nightcap; the gown billows up revealing his nearly naked self beneath . . . coming straight at the boy! He appears to be achieving almost terminal velocity and, when he reaches the base, goes flying out across the lab, tucking himself into a ball and rolling right up to the boy's feet. He has placed a huge, goose-down pillow on the floor, set in just the right spot to cushion such falls.

But Sherlock's master isn't fooling him. He has slid down the railing because walking the stairs has become painful. Yesterday, Holmes found the old man's handkerchief shoved under a mattress, spotted with red spit and phlegm. Over the last six months, Bell's cough has become frightening, the sound in his chest like a death rattle. But he never speaks of it, never shows the least bit of concern.

"Why are you up at this hour, my young knight?" he inquires, sitting below Sherlock on the floor. The boy reaches down, takes his old, thin hand, and helps raise him to his feet.

"No reason, sir."

"That is not what I taught you to –"

"There is always a reason," sighs Sherlock.

"Yes. There is. One must search for it, encounter it, and grapple with it!"

"I cannot grapple with anything anymore, sir."

Sigerson Bell's shining eyes barely hide the worry underneath. Ever since he met the boy, he has been able to pull him up from his depressions. A violent joust of Bellitsu, during which they nearly break each other's bones, a dangerous chemical experiment punctuated with an explosion or two, or a violin lesson in the more obscure movements of the great Paganini have always done the trick. But nothing has worked for six months. The old man knows exactly why.

Worst of all was the death of Wilberforce Holmes, not long before Christmas. That, however, was just one blow, just the hardest punch in a series of assaults upon the boy's well-being. His hero, Benjamin Disraeli, the miraculous Jewish Prime Minister of the Empire, was defeated in the country's last election; Irene Doyle, the love of his life, has been in America now for nine months, abandoning him for stage and voice training in New York City, her once-daily letters slowed to a trickle; and Beatrice Leckie, the poor hatter's daughter with the sparkling black eyes and genuine concern for him, appears to have found someone else to give her the attention she once sought from him. More dangerous than all, he has been trying, once again, to keep out of criminal investigations. He is just a boy, he reasons, he needs to grow, to arm himself better. But this inaction is killing him from the inside out.

"Shall we eat, my boy? Headcheese? Blood pudding? Stewed turnips?"

Even those delectable meals can't stir him. He sits facing straight ahead, his gray eyes looking all pupil and nearly black.

To the north, only a few blocks away, a small young man sits on the floor of his gloomy bedroom, weeping. He is dark haired and dark eyed, his age difficult to distinguish; he hasn't grown in years. He hates many people, but Sherlock Holmes is his most despised.

"He doesn't know what I 'ave endured," he whimpers. "The boss doesn't *really* know either. I should kill them both, I should. I deserves more."

He had been left at a workhouse doorstep as a baby and raised inside its black stone walls, eating its gruel twice a day, taking rudimentary reading classes at a Ragged School, smarter somehow than the others, but torn away from the workhouse at the age of ten and put into the streets. He cost too much to keep.

"I were clever in schooling!" he cries. He sniffles and stops his sobbing with a great effort of will. Then he shouts, "I 'ave an opportunity, NOW, I does!"

His house has no furniture but his bed. He only ever has one visitor. He looks at the clothes that have been purchased for him, lying in a pile nearby: respectable suits, cravats, and waistcoats; black leather gloves, a bowler hat, and an umbrella. In the morning, he will comb his hair as he has been taught, clean his face, put on the boots he has been told to polish.

"The boss is 'iding something from me! I will find what it is. I will 'ave more than just this job 'e is making me do!"

He has fought Sherlock Holmes many times, sometimes in desperate combats down on the cobblestones, instructed by his leader. He remembers those struggles, how he had wanted to do something terrible to the half-Jew. If he'd been allowed a knife, he would have driven it deep into Holmes's breastbone and through his heart. He remembers the good boy panting beneath him, squirming, and treasures the memory of that fear. But Holmes is not such easy prey anymore. He has been taught how to fight, has lethal skills a strange apothecary has shown him.

It would be best to not fight fair with him, thinks the little man. That is *always* best.

"Someday soon, I will finish 'im!"

Sherlock takes a long time to respond to Sigerson Bell's invitation to eat. His mind is far away. He is thinking about Malefactor. Holmes could use the excitement of a confrontation with that blackguard now. In fact, he needs it. But Malefactor has become a shadow too, scheming somewhere, planning even bigger things. A year ago, the crook had said that he was turning respectable. Sherlock knew what that meant. Greater evil was coming. His villainous lieutenants, Grimsby and Crew, have vanished with him.

To the west, in a beautiful home, a wealthy man lies awake. He sees two monsters when he closes his eyes, monsters he loves. But someone *knows*. Some fiend, some shadow he cannot lay his hand upon, told him by letter what would be done if "arrangements" were not made. And so, he had used his influence to put a worthless human being with perhaps evil intent into a place he does not belong, into a position of power. And the villain who engineered this is still plotting.

That enemy is far away in a respectable place, a spider spinning a web. At least once a day, he says to himself with a snarl, "Stay out of this, Sherlock Holmes."

Holmes became an orphan suddenly, in his mind, though he should not have thought that. Kind Beatrice had pushed him to renew his relationship with his father, and they had set aside their grief and Sherlock's guilt about his mother's murder and had begun seeing each other. His father had been growing thinner with every visit, but the boy had chosen to ignore it. When Beatrice's frantic thumping sounded on the apothecary's entrance on a cold December night, he knew what had happened. He opened the door and saw her standing in a snowstorm, the jingle of carriages behind her, a gaslight glowing down on her as though she were an angel, but her black eyes filled with tears. Word had been sent to the hatter's shop: a paralytic stroke had taken his father from him.

The funeral, at a respectable church in Sydenham and paid for by the old man's Crystal Palace employer, brought few mourners. Sherlock sat between Beatrice and Bell, down a pew from his older brother – Mycroft was seven years his senior and had left home long ago. They had seldom seen each other since.

Holmes had wept uncontrollably and was horribly embarrassed. Beatrice had attempted to take his arm but he had pulled away, trying to stiffen his upper lip. Bell knew not to interfere. The boy had risen from his place and moved nearer Mycroft, and that, for some reason, had helped him stifle his emotions. As the service went on, he drew comfort from his older brother's presence, though they never once looked at each other. Mycroft didn't shed a tear, but as they were leaving, he noticed the redness in his younger brother's eyes.

"Well, Sherlock, it has been a pleasure to see you. If it is orphans we are to be, then orphans we are. Oliver Twist made out all right." Then he paused. "Uh, you may come to see me, if you please, at the office. It would be a . . . pleasure. Send your card first." And with that, he was off.

Mycroft Holmes has no *real* interest in seeing his brother at this time in his life. Perhaps in the future, when the pain of their childhood, the stain of their "half-breed" origins, and the trauma of their parents' deaths have faded, they could become friends. Had the boy ever appeared near Mycroft's tiny office at Her Majesty's Treasury, that ominous stone structure where the nation's money is controlled, the older brother would have nearly fainted from the sight.

But as Sherlock sits at the lab table, he desperately needs friendship. There are pains in his chest, and he feels a shortness of breath. It is as if he were slowly being squeezed to death.

To the south that morning, a ship unloads its cargo on the smelly docks of the River Thames. It has come from South America. A red-haired man awaits its most precious passenger. But it isn't human. The man smiles when he sees it. He has just emerged from a prison himself. A strange thought flickers through his mind, a magical one.

"What if I unleashed this thing?" It makes him smile, and then his smile broadens. "What if I set it upon Sherlock Holmes?"

"Sir, I don't feel much like eating," says Sherlock to Sigerson Bell. As he does, his eyes rest on the newspapers with their black headlines. "I cannot believe that!"

"Yes, well, you know, Dickens was not God."

"Probably not."

"Though he wrote like Him, told us about life, real life. He was a little like Mercury."

"A messenger?"

"Indeed, but a very human one for someone with an Olympian ear, a flawed chap, I hear. Had a mistress and a temper and could be rather cold."

"We are all flawed, deeply flawed. There is so much evil –"

"You are such a sunny chap, my boy. Might you say something, *anything*, that is not sad, just once!"

Sigerson Bell's voice is rising, his face turning red. But then he begins to cough and cannot stop. It rumbles in his lungs and growls in his larynx and something comes up his throat. He reaches for a handkerchief and catches it, wrapping the cloth close to his mouth, but not close enough to hide the red liquid that escapes.

"And now *this*!" cries Sherlock, staring at the handkerchief.

The old man stops coughing instantly. He glares at his ward. "I have had enough of you, Sherlock Holmes, you and your concern for yourself! The world changes, my boy. People die and others are born. The only constant is change! We must face it like men! Do you think that Charles Dickens groaned about in his chair all day, bemoaning his fate? No, he got on with it! He worked! If you do not stop this, you shall expire before you are a help to anyone! If you keep up these black moods, they shall plague you all your life!"

"What would you have me do?" says the boy, and for

the first time in his life he speaks to Sigerson Bell with sarcasm dripping from his words.

"I would have you get up off your arse!"

"My arse?"

"Before I kick it from here to Buckingham Palace!"

"You . . . you are right, sir. I have things to do here today."

"No! You do not!"

"I do not?"

"You are going out that door! Leave me! Now!"

With that, the old man actually seizes the boy by his collar, raises him to his feet, and kicks him in the arse. Sherlock almost runs to the door and out. As he stands under a gaslight on the foot pavement on Denmark Street, a few working-class folk rushing past in the still-dark morning, he can't reach down and summon any courage. He still feels sorry for himself. His master has literally kicked him out. Will he ever welcome him back? Sherlock feels dead inside – absolutely alone and unloved.

So, he makes up his mind to do something he never dreamed he would. Unable to return to the shop, he decides to go to Whitehall to Her Majesty's Treasury, the Office of the Chancellor of the Exchequer, to see the only living person who shares his very blood, who might care for him.

Back in the apothecary shop, Sigerson Bell begins to cough again. This time, the red sputum almost fills his handkerchief.

Sherlock slouches down Denmark Street toward central London and the river, passing those imaginary black mourning ribbons on shops, early folk on their way to workplaces, and newsboys scurrying toward their accustomed spots with bundles of papers in their arms, ready to shout the news of Dickens's funeral arrangements to the masses.

Holmes is six feet tall now, and his voice has dropped an octave since January. *Next year, I will be seventeen years old, and the following season, by hook or by crook, studying at a university. Then, I can pursue my calling.* But as he walks, a chilling feeling descends upon him. He wonders if he will ever achieve his dreams. *Death is not just nearby*, he thinks, *it is fast approaching me.* He *knows* it. It is like a message from God.

To the east, north, west, and south, Sherlock Holmes's enemies are awake and plotting.

Everything is about to change, forever.

2

THE NEW MAN AT THE TREASURY

Sherlock Holmes has made the trip from the shop to Whitehall Street many times. It takes him south down modest Crown Street past a granite workhouse, into bustling Trafalgar Square, and then along the river to that famous wide street with its government buildings. But he usually stops before he gets to the offices that line it, all tall and imposing, mostly white and stone, the Prime Minister's residence and Westminster Palace nearby. His destination is usually where sprawling Scotland Yard sits tucked back from the thoroughfare, and he often approaches from the north side to be inconspicuous. Inspector Lestrade likes to have him chased away. But as Sherlock looks across at police headquarters today, he actually smiles. His opponent has recently retired, making room for a place at the bottom of the detective pole for his ambitious son.

The boy contemplates young Lestrade for a moment. *Is he the one?* Would he be that one male companion that Sherlock needs in life, helping him fight crime? He dismisses the idea. Lestrade will be a conventional detective, his methods those of his father and the unimaginative Force.

I must be an irregular, independent, my ways new and daring; illegal, if need be.

At this very minute, the little man in the barren house to the north, the villain with the murderous thoughts, is putting on his strange clothing for the day. He too will soon walk south toward Whitehall. He has no mirror with which to examine his adjusted appearance. But he doesn't care. He knows he is ugly, even in these respectable clothes. Any joy he gets from life never comes from his appearance but from what he can do to others, what he can gain by cunning and brutality. But this morning an awful feeling is overwhelming him. When he looks through his windows, he also sees the imaginary dark ribbons on the buildings outside. He worries about what the boss has asked him to do, and feels his days are numbered. Death is all around him too.

Big Ben chimes five. More working-class folk are on the streets now: milk women, dustmen, charwomen, costermongers readying their wares on two-wheeled wagons, grooms driving horse and carriages, and humble people in the uniforms of the domestic service. Sherlock dares to sit for a moment on the steps of the Admiralty. The fog has not entirely lifted yet.

What will become of me when Mr. Bell dies? If young Lestrade can't be my confidant, then who can be? Not a woman; I cannot put her in danger. It should be someone clever, though not as ingenious as me, for I must make myself smarter than the encyclopedias on the shop shelves. A man skilled in science, yes, with some courage, who would listen to me, ordinary but not too ordinary; loyal and dedicated to my cause, but with his own profession. I must be the boss. An idea comes to him. *What about a writer? One who could record my cases, spread my fame, and frighten criminals. Doesn't that make sense?* He balks at it. *I cannot do this for fame.* But then he reconsiders. *What if he wasn't a real writer, just a direct man who can tell the truth?*

Further thoughts are arrested by the sight of his brother waddling up Whitehall toward him in suit and cravat, tall top hat on his head, walking stick pacing the foot pavement, also deep in thought. A little pudgy and over six feet tall, he is the first respectable man Sherlock has seen.

"Mycroft?"

His older brother almost falls over at the sight of him.

"Sherlock? I . . . I . . ."

"You are early."

"Yes, well, the early bird gets the worm, especially if such an ornithological creature is of half-Hebraic heritage and worms are not offered to him. What are you doing here?"

"You said you would host a visit from me."

Mycroft glances up and down the street. None of his colleagues are in sight yet. "Yes, I did, didn't I? I suppose you never *actually* send round your card first?"

"Shall we go in?"

"Well, perhaps . . . not yet. There is a lovely establishment nearby that will give us morning tea. Shall we?" He gestures down the street. Big Ben has not yet chimed six.

They are soon huddled together at a small table in an inn, all wood and cigar smoke and ale, uncomfortably close to one another. Sherlock loves to apply penetrating stares to suspects to break down their identities, but neither he nor his brother is given to looking into the other's eyes. If the younger sibling is searching for someone with whom to commiserate, he has come to the wrong man. Mycroft is brisk in his manner and evasive of anything like warm emotions. He introduces the subject of their parents immediately, as if to deal with it and be done with it, mentioning that, statistically, they have been orphaned at an advanced age and have nothing to complain about. It makes Sherlock feel as though he has been acting and thinking like a coward. Still, he cannot shake his sense of impending doom, but he tries to control it.

"I must say that I am impressed with your ambition to be a professional fighter of crime."

"You are?"

"Indeed. A career in the police department is admirable."

"I will not be a policeman."

"Pardon me? Surely this stumbling about on your own

and helping to collar the odd bad man independently is not a way to proceed professionally."

Sherlock has revealed few details to him about his cases. As far as his brother knows, he was very much on the periphery of such investigations as the Whitechapel murder, the Rathbone kidnapping, and the Hemsworth-Nottingham affair.

"It was more than stumbling about."

"But, Sherlock, you are a mere child."

"I am sixteen years old. I am almost ready to become a professional."

"No more schooling?"

"I am preparing for university. I hope to attend somewhere, and then return to London."

"University? That will be tricky."

"I have a plan, God willing."

"God willing? Concerned about mortality at your age, are you, Sherlock?"

"One never knows."

"But why do you need higher education? Surely police training will be enough for –"

"I told you, I do not want to be a policeman. I hope to be a detective."

"Yes, well, the Force has a department for that now, you know."

"A private detective, a consulting one."

"Private? Consulting? Never heard of –"

"An irregular; I must do what others cannot."

"You are ambitious, Sherlock."

"And you are not?"

"I will do what a half-Jew must do to have influence. I will rise quietly and subtly, but rise nevertheless, at the seat of real power."

"The Chancellor of the Exchequer?"

"To start with; then I will find my way upward in other departments even more important to our empire's policy and security. But the Treasury, you know, is in charge of the money. Control that, and you control a great deal." He smiles.

Mycroft had begun as an errand boy. Just as brilliant and ambitious as Sherlock, he intends to one day pull important strings from behind the scenes. Unlike his younger brother, he has no appetite for attention.

They sink into silence and find it difficult to know what to say to each other. Despite what they have in common in terms of brains, drive, and blood, there is little they can share when it comes to small talk. They sip their tea awkwardly, seeking the bottom of their last cups.

The little man who dreams of killing Sherlock Holmes is approaching, making his way to work well ahead of arrival time, as he has been told to do. He is thinking about his boss. "He 'as big plans this time, 'e does, biggest ever," he murmurs out loud. "There's something behind it that 'e is keeping from me. There's a murder 'e is planning too, very soon, I figures. But 'e won't let me do it; 'e'll let Crew. Fat pig."

Back at morning tea in Whitehall, Sherlock offers his older brother a question to kill the final few moments of their get-together.

"And so, how goes the business of the Treasury?"

"In the black, my boy, and running like clockwork. Speaking of which, I must be getting back." He gets to his feet.

"And *you,* Mycroft, how are you making out in your own particular corner there?"

"Everything according to plan; I have my own office now."

Mycroft drops a few coins on the little table and ushers Sherlock out the door. The bell tinkles as they leave.

"So, no worries?"

"No, Sherlock, none, though I cannot say that for all my colleagues."

"Oh?"

"There have been a few surprising dismissals of late." They turn the corner into Whitehall Street and walk at a brisk pace. The magnificent Treasury building nears, tall and long, pillared and elegant. "And the dismissed have been replaced by especially surprising chaps."

There is still half a block to go.

"What do you mean by that?"

"Well, one young man, whose qualifications I must say I doubt, has been placed in a rather delicate and powerful role at the Treasury for a new employee. He shall have some say over funds allocated to the London police; this, right off the hop, to a neophyte. I find it bloody dangerous."

"Curious."

"Indeed," Mycroft frowns. "His superior is an elderly man, and this young fellow is one of several who could have his position soon! He could exercise some control over our police force within a year or so." Inwardly, Sherlock is smiling, enjoying his big brother's evident jealousy. They say nothing for the next minute, their pace increasing, Mycroft's walking stick leading them quickly toward the Treasury's front steps.

"Ah!" he says suddenly, looking away just as Sherlock is hoping he will extend his hand to shake good-bye. He lowers his voice. "There he is! The very man!"

Mycroft is motioning with a nod of his head to someone walking briskly up the wide stone steps. It is barely seven o'clock, so this fellow is obviously ambitious too, almost as driven as one Mycroft Holmes.

Sherlock looks across at the man. He is very short but wears a pin-striped suit with cravat, a black bowler hat, black hair greased back underneath, and new spectacles glistening in the mid-June morning sun. He sports black kid gloves, sparkling black shoes, and carries an expensive umbrella, though there is little evidence of threatening rain. The suit is slightly ill-fitting and somehow hangs uncomfortably on him. It is almost as if he were wearing a costume. The little man notices that he is being observed. He turns and looks directly at the Holmes brothers. When he does, Sherlock nearly collapses.

It is Grimsby!

3

HIS WAY IN

The boy is too stunned to say another word to his brother. He takes Mycroft's hand and shakes it, not even hearing his farewell, then stumbles away. He needs to talk to someone he can trust about this, *now*. There is only one person in whom he can confide.

But will Sigerson Bell even let him back into his shop?

The apothecary is actually waiting at the door, peeking out the window, then pacing, wringing his hands, aghast that he actually thrust his dear boy out the door, literally kicking him in his arse. He is praying for his return. "I should not have been so cantankerous! So curmudgeonly! So supercilious!" he mutters. The sight of the boy through the bulging latticed windows nearly makes him jump up and down. He flings open the door. Sherlock has been wondering if he should knock. They begin apologizing to each other simultaneously. It arrests them into silence. The old man looks longingly into the boy's eyes and immediately sees something there, a light trying to emerge under the sadness.

"Aha!" cries Bell.

"Aha?"

"You are stimulated by something!"

"Yes, well, something decidedly odd has happened, *very* odd indeed."

"Step into my laboratory and we shall converse!"

Moments later Sherlock has reacquainted the old man with just exactly who Grimsby is and the fact that he now appears to be employed by the Chancellor of the Exchequer to help oversee funds allocated to the Metropolitan London Police. The apothecary knows that Holmes deeply despises the little street thug, and not just because he is his great enemy's lieutenant.

"Ah, he has his hands on our taxes! I must say, a rather meteoric rise from thieving in the streets of London to thieving for the government!" Bell grins. "He has switched positions. He is now stealing from the poor to give to the rich!"

"Sir, I don't think we should treat this lightly."

"Of course not," says the apothecary, feeling a little sheepish.

"I smell a rat."

"I would pluralize that! There is a rather larger one at work here too, boss to this Grimsby, who used to live on the streets with his fellow Rodentia, exceeding six feet tall and wearing a tailcoat."

"Indeed."

"But Malefactor has disappeared. You haven't seen him for nearly a year and then only briefly. He spoke of attending a university, did he not? Becoming respectable?"

"In order to be more effective."

"It appears that is now the case. He is infiltrating our government! But this Grimsby chap is not too highly placed yet, is he?"

"He may be second in command."

"Second? Oh dear. Well, at least he isn't first."

But Sherlock Holmes doesn't respond. A sudden, disturbing thought has overcome him. *What if Grimsby's elderly superior were to soon meet with an unfortunate accident?* Malefactor could get one of his thugs to make that happen with ease, without a whiff of suspicion. *They WILL make that happen.* Sherlock has a burning desire to run to the Treasury, throw Grimsby to the ground, disable him, and force from him whatever secrets he and his evil boss are holding. *The infiltration of the police force will be preceded by murder.* The boy is becoming aware that these things are not simply future dreams in Malefactor's teeming brain. *They are at hand.*

"Someone should look into this," says Sigerson Bell, glancing away.

"Yes, someone should." Sherlock's voice is shaking.

Bell turns back and observes his charge. He can see the color changing in his face. He notices his hands twitching by his sides, turning into fists.

"You, my young knight, could make enquiries. Just enquiries, mind you. You are at a unique advantage to do so, with your brother holding an inside position, as it were."

"I suppose I am." Sherlock's mind is racing. "Just enquiries," he says quietly, his hands now so tightly clenched that the bones show through his knuckles.

If I let Malefactor do this, he will soon infest everything. This is his way in. He will then destroy everyone who dares to oppose him, including me.

4

GRIMSBY'S RISE

When Sherlock gets to Whitehall Street very early the next morning, he sees a long line of people, going west along the thoroughfare, starting on the far side of the Treasury building and growing by the minute. The sun is just peeking over the foggy streets. Folk of all stripes are in the line, no one pushing or shoving. They are rich, middle class, and poor, but mostly poor. People of such different incomes never gather together in England. Many carry flowers, and all look sad. Some are shoeless and ill, clutching wilted weeds tied up with rags. The line stretches out of sight, half a mile into the distance toward Westminster Abbey. They are lining up to walk past Charles Dickens's coffin in the great church. Many of the poor are crying so hard that their shoulders are shaking.

Sherlock would like to join them, but there are things he must do today, an evil he *must* immediately root out. He wonders if Malefactor would kill so soon after inserting Grimsby. It doesn't seem like a smart move. *But he is likely flushed with excitement and anxious to act. How long until he strikes? Will it be weeks? Or just a few days?*

Sherlock waits anxiously on the front steps of the Treasury. He knows exactly when to be here, this time. Sure enough, just before six o'clock, Mycroft Holmes appears, coming from the same direction as yesterday, glancing at the snaking Dickens line-up, and just as shocked as before to see his sibling awaiting him.

"Ah," he says with a suspicious look in his eye, "what a pleasure to see you on two consecutive days. What an absolute pleasure." His younger brother looks as if he hasn't slept.

"Dispense with the lies, sir. I have come to tell you something and ask you a few questions."

"And they are?"

"I must admit that I was shaken by the sight of the new Treasury employee, whom you referred to at tea with some concern, who then miraculously appeared on these very steps."

"And why is that?"

"I know him."

"You know him? Then I was indeed correct about his hiding his low accent. Does a rather poor job of it, I must say. His origins are as a working-class man, or am I deceived?"

"You are not. He is working class, indeed!"

"You say that with some feeling."

"He is a scoundrel and thief. He has somehow raised himself from –"

"My! There he is now! Goodness, he is coming even earlier today. It is as if he were trying to compete with me."

Mycroft is looking over Sherlock's shoulder as he speaks. "Ronald?" he calls out and waves for the Treasury's new employee to join them.

"Ronald?" says Sherlock. He turns and sees Grimsby coming to a halt. Their eyes meet.

"Yes, Ronald Loveland." Mycroft lowers his voice. "I am sure he is not as bad as you say. Perhaps you and he had some disagreements in the past, but calling him a scoundrel and a thief, my boy, that is rather dramatic. One must get over one's personal squabbles. I have reservations about him too, as you know, but he will likely do fine. One must not disparage one's colleagues. It isn't good form."

Grimsby isn't moving.

Mycroft calls out. "Ronald, you must come forward and meet my brother, Sherlock Holmes." He leans toward Sherlock and lowers his voice again. "I am glad you have washed your horrible frock coat since yesterday, my boy, though by its condition, it looks as if you wash it most every day. You should get more sleep too. You must say hello to my colleague right *here,* out of doors, and I am afraid that you must then depart. Thank God it is still early. There aren't too many others around yet. Let us do this quickly."

Grimsby still hasn't moved. Sherlock can see his villainous black eyes looking unsure beneath his disguise – under his glasses, his black bowler hat, slicked hair, and fancy suit. Holmes thinks of others like Grimsby he has dealt with, how this one is among the worst, a sort of symbol of evil for him, a cowardly little devil but capable of so much painful mischief. He remembers the beatings Grimsby tried to inflict upon him, his desire to hurt him, break his bones, and disfigure him. He is a little sadist with dark ambitions.

Sherlock turns and quickly advances toward him.

"Sherlock?" says his brother.

Holmes almost runs to the little man. Grimsby flinches.

"You will keep your distance, sir." He points his walking stick at him.

It is Grimsby's voice, indeed, though he is struggling to make the accent sound respectable.

"You will keep your distance!"

Holmes seizes him by the lapels.

"SHERLOCK!" cries Mycroft.

"I do not know how you came to this employment," whispers the tall, thin boy, inches from his enemy's ear, "but I know it is for no good. I know what you are planning. I shall discover how you got here and use that to put an end to it!"

Mycroft begins running toward them.

"You, 'olmes, shall do naught of the kind," hisses Grimsby as quietly as possible, turning his face so his lips are an inch from Sherlock's. "Things is in motion now that is well beyond you, well beyond the little games we used to play. HE is making plans. They is developing. If you do not cease this 'ere scene, it is you who will be in grave danger in a wink."

"I am quivering in my hobnail boots."

"If you lays a finger upon me, you will be murdered before you reach your little apothecary shop."

"I don't care what –"

"And your apothecary with you. Perhaps I shall do that myself?"

Sherlock hesitates. Mycroft arrives.

"What is this about, Sherlock? My God, unhand him!"

Sherlock releases Grimsby's lapels.

"No worries," says Grimsby in his awkward new voice. "This is just a misunderstanding, a case of mistaken identity." He smiles at Sherlock. "Isn't it, sir?"

Sherlock says nothing.

"Well, Ronald, my brother is rather impulsive, shall we say, and not as serious-minded as those in our profession. You may see this by his dress. But he is a good lad, inside."

"I am sure. Pleased to make your acquaintance, sir." Grimsby extends a hand. "Ronald Loveland, at your service!" He keeps his lips closed when he smiles, hiding his pointed, yellow teeth.

Sherlock hesitates again. He looks down at the ugly little hand. The fingernails aren't groomed as they should be. In fact, he sees dirt under them and wretched red cuticles that look as though they are still being gnawed, just as they were when the two first met.

"Well, Sherlock, take his hand."

Sherlock shakes it as limply as possible. It feels wet and cold. The fingers are short and stubby. Grimsby is still smiling at him. "Good day," he says, lifting his bowler and bowing slightly. He has used too much oil in his hair. He rushes up the steps to the Treasury.

"Sherlock!" cries Mycroft as soon as Grimsby has gone. "You cannot do this to me!"

"He is who I say he is. He has designs you cannot imagine. They will be enacted soon."

"I shall repeat: one must get over one's personal squabbles. It is beneath even you to carry a grudge and to manifest it in such words as 'thief' and 'scoundrel.'"

"I know him to be, quite literally, what I say he is. Just a year or so ago he was upon the streets running with a gang, getting his living by criminal means, one of two lieutenants to the most heinous and successful young thug in London, a regrettably brilliant villain who has now left the sewers to further his career of crime by hiding his true intentions in a cloak of respectability. That leader, who calls himself Malefactor, has ambitions of a leviathan sort. He has the faculties and the passion to someday dominate this city's, perhaps this country's, perhaps this continent's, criminal world. At this very moment, he is trying, via this ugly little man, to lay his hand upon the police."

"But this is preposterous. Ronald Loveland? You can't be serious . . . can you?"

"There is no doubt. Under that bowler hat, those spectacles and suit, he is an animal named Grimsby."

"Grimsby? But how could this happen?"

"An excellent question."

"Perhaps he isn't associated with this chap you mention anymore? Perhaps he has reformed?"

"Grimsby does not reform. Had you heard what he said to me under his breath, you would know that to be true."

Mycroft pauses. "Well, we Holmeses may be many things, but we are not liars, not mendacious sorts."

"I am not lying."

"That is what I am saying. I believe you."

"Thank you." Sherlock almost smiles.

"Or at least I believe that *you* believe it to be true. And if you are right, even somewhat right, this must be looked into."

"A crime is being planned, Mycroft, and after that, there will be many more. If we do not put a stop to this, Grimsby will be just the first invisible germ – much like the kind the queen's physician Dr. Snow speaks of and Sigerson Bell believes in too, that gets into people's physical systems and destroys their health – that will infect not just our police force but our very government for many years to come. We must cure it now!"

"Not *we*, my dear Sherlock; perhaps *you*, but not *we*. This is not my game. But I will tell you what I know. Father always said the most important thing to do at the beginning of a scientific problem –"

"Was to ask the right questions."

"Absolutely. And the question you must answer at the outset is: *Exactly* how did this young thief, if he indeed is so, come by this job? That is your first move."

"I have no doubt that Malefactor is behind it."

"Well, I do not know of anyone by that name making decisions for the Chancellor of the Exchequer," quips Mycroft.

"No, I am sure it did not work that way. He has done it in some brilliant and secretive manner, behind the scenes."

Mycroft glances up and down the frontage of the Treasury. There are still few fellow employees about. He speaks more softly.

"I can tell you that appointments in the Treasury are made by upper civil servants; the lower the position, the lower the civil servant who does the hiring. The upper positions, the important jobs, are filled directly by a committee, rather than the Chancellor."

"Mr. Robert Lowe."

"Yes, the albino genius himself, a favorite of Prime Minister Gladstone's and said to be ruthless."

"But is he crooked? Could he be bribed?"

"I doubt it, not Mr. Lowe. He is too ambitious and in love with himself. He would not allow a stain upon his character. And as I say, he employs a committee to make the highest appointments anyway, so there is no appearance of favoritism. The hiring of Loveland is a middling one, but not insignificant. The committee might or might not have done it."

"Who serves on that committee?"

"A small roster of respectable financial figures."

"Chaired by whom?"

"The Governor of the Bank of England, Sir Ramsay Stonefield."

"Could he reach his hand down as far as the position that our little Grimsby holds and see to it that a certain someone had it?"

"I don't see why he would."

"But *could* he?"

"I suppose, but again, *why* would he?"

"Yes, why would he?" says Sherlock, deep in thought. Then he shakes himself awake and takes his brother by the hand. His eyes are brighter than they have been for almost a year. "You have been most helpful. I wish you good day, sir, and hope to have some news for you before long."

Mycroft smiles. "You have little to go on from what I can see, Sherlock, mostly an inchoate theory, but I wish you well. I must admit, this problem of yours amuses me. I shall betray nothing of my knowledge to one Ronald Loveland, since he may ask about you. In fact, I shall put him off your scent entirely. I shall tell him that I have browbeaten you unmercifully for confronting him and you are going home at this very instant with your tail between your legs, which is a falsehood in every detail, since you, sir, are chuffed and heading *east*, I deduce. All the best to you!"

The brothers part and don't look back – Mycroft up the steps to the Treasury building and his office, and Sherlock back along Whitehall to Trafalgar Square and then east to the Old City and the Bank of England's magnificent headquarters on Threadneedle Street.

I must discover what got him that job, and then the rest will unfold.

At that very moment, Grimsby is summoning a boy to his desk. He is writing him a note to be delivered to an educational institute a good distance from London. It begins with the words, "Sherlock Holmes . . ."

5

THE GOVERNOR

Sherlock, of course, has already formed a plan. He will arrive at the great bank about half an hour before it opens. That will be perfect. He isn't tutoring at school today, so he can do as he pleases. He moves quickly. When he reaches Fleet Street, passing by the offices of famous newspapers, all with black Dickens headlines displayed in their windows, pedestrian and carriage traffic has picked up considerably. The air smells of horse manure and burning coal, human sweat and urine. Wagons and hansom cabs and omnibuses jam the street, reins jingling, wheels grinding on cobblestones, thousands of hoof beats clacking, pedestrians somehow finding their way through a flowing crowd of vehicles, while drivers shout at their steeds. Up the hill ahead sits St. Paul's Cathedral, where he once secretly met Irene during the Whitechapel murder case. He dashes that memory from his mind, concentrating on making his way through the river of people. It is a weekday, and London is about to truly hum. Partway up Ludgate Hill, he passes the remnants of the London Wall and enters the Old City. This is where the Romans lived and England now operates its financial institutions. Sherlock straightens his second-hand frock coat, runs his hand through his black hair to make sure it is in place, and swings north to Cheapside. From here he soon sees the Lord Mayor's home at the intersection of three ancient City streets. These arteries are narrow and tight with wonderful old buildings towering along the little foot pavements, built during another time when people were smaller, transportation slower, and vehicles far fewer in number.

And there on the north side near the Stock Exchange sits the building he is seeking, the Old Lady of Threadneedle Street. It is three stories high, interminably long and fronted with pillars, taking up an entire block. Inside these walls, in its elegant rooms and under its impressive domes, grinds the engine of the Empire's finances. The Bank of England is the most important bank in the world, setting the standard for the nation and the pace for all other countries too. The value of the pound, it is said, is based upon the amount of gold in its vaults.

Sherlock's mission is not to speak to the Governor or even have someone do that for him. That is not remotely possible. He merely wants to see him. From that, other things can unfold. *One must start with something, anything, and build from there.* Observation, both his father and Sigerson Bell have taught him, is the alpha and the omega of confronting a problem. But one must do it thoroughly and correctly.

He knows that he is in pursuit of a secret. The employment of Grimsby at Her Majesty's Treasury has come from one, perhaps from a series. He is sure of it. It is a move begun in the shadows. Holmes has deduced that the insertion of an unqualified unknown into a position of some power, however elementary, *had* to have come through one of two men: the Chancellor of the Exchequer or the Governor of the Bank of England. The former, Mr. Robert Lowe, as Mycroft has informed him, is not the sort to be bribed or used, no matter the circumstances. *But what of the Governor?*

Holmes is here to use his already consummate powers of observation, born of his genetics and honed by his father and his brilliant (though decidedly eccentric) apothecary master, to find clues evolving from mere glances, seconds of observation. Over the past three years, he has been training his talents to a fine edge. He senses that the time has come, as Malefactor's lieutenant stands just a man or two away from influence in police and financial affairs, to use all of the skills and the knowledge he now has at his command. He hopes that they are enough because, almost overnight, a pivotal moment has arrived.

But secrets must be cleverly approached: by cover of crowds, distance, or disguise.

Big Ben had chimed eight just as he reached Fleet Street, so he is guessing it is nearing half past the hour. He walks to the front of the majestic building and up to the oval opening within which are set the mammoth front doors. It is guarded by liveried men. A crowd has formed. It is too early for customers to be queuing. These people are waiting for something else, for someone else. Sherlock surveys them. They are all men. He concentrates: they are all businessmen too. He observes their clothing, the expressions on their faces. They are dressed to impress, many uncomfortable in Sunday clothes they seldom wear, hair over-groomed, top hats too high and rented for the day. He zeroes in on their eyes, their lips. He sees the latter moving slightly, rehearsing lines like actors. Sherlock turns to the street. Hansom cabs and carriages were lining the front of the building as the boy approached, but now he sees a half-dozen Bobbies moving vehicles from the area directly in front of the doors.

Sherlock smiles. He has timed it perfectly. He knows what is about to happen. He must wait here for as long as it takes. The Governor of the Bank of England is about to arrive for the day. The great man will descend from his carriage in this very spot cleared by the police and will be deluged by requests for help from these businessmen. He will respond to none. But Sherlock Holmes, now moving into position, will see him, up close, even if just for a fleeting moment. He hopes that is all his developing powers will need.

It happens as he suspected.

Just as the minute arm on the big clock, which he can see inside the front doors of the bank, reaches six, Sir Ramsay Stonefield appears. But at first, that is all that goes according to plan. The very moment the ornate carriage arrives, the crowd of supplicants moves forward like hounds attempting to tree a fox. The Bobbies strain to hold them back, and Sherlock is caught in the midst of the mob, barely able to see his target. They shout out their needs.

"Sir Ramsay, I have a business plan!"

"I simply need a modest loan!"

"Sir Ramsay, my relations are well placed!"

But the Governor of the Bank of England magnificently ignores them. Every one-in-a-million opportunity falls on deaf ears. His liveried footman, dressed in red family colors and white stockings, leaps down from the back of their shining black conveyance and opens the door. The man himself descends from the carriage looking glum, as if he is already disgruntled with his day. He places his incredibly tall stovepipe top hat upon his head, runs his fingers down his golden chain to extricate his pocket watch from his pin-striped waistcoat, glances at it, and then snaps it shut.

"Spot on, James!" he announces to his driver. "Now clear these citizens from my path!" He waves his walking stick at the Bobbies and then the crowd.

Glimpsing him between heads and armpits and waving hats, Sherlock observes what he can. First, the accent: *London born, Mayfair or Knightsbridge, Oxford educated, Balliol College.* Clothes: *Savile Row tailor, ostentatious without boasting.* Age: *fifty-five or -six but looking ten years older.* Attitude: *Fastidious, meticulous, concerned about being on time and on schedule.* Expression: *Sad, preoccupied.* Sir Ramsay turns back to the carriage as if he has forgotten something. He asks his footman to open the door again. Sherlock can see a woman inside, about the great man's age. Stonefield appears, for a moment, as if he might kiss her, but stops. He waves. She weakly waves back. And then, in a walk (and one's gait speaks volumes) that is intended to be brisk but takes much effort to be so, he goes up the steps and indoors.

Sherlock has learned a great deal. But the appearance of the Governor's wife, obviously Lady Stonefield from the cut and material of her clothing, and curiously with him on his morning trip to work, has the potential to tell him much more. As the others race after the Governor, the boy rushes the other way, to the carriage, and purposely stumbles so as to land, face against the glass, just before the carriage departs. He sees the Governor's wife, all alone, an expression of extreme sadness upon her face. Under her black bonnet, she stares out the other window, looking like the loneliest woman in the world.

"Get away from there, you swine!" calls the footman from the carriage's runners behind, about to leap down and manhandle Sherlock Holmes. The driver turns at the same instant and looks as though he wants to use his whip on the boy.

"I beg your pardon, sirs!" cries Sherlock and jumps back. The carriage wheels away.

But Holmes is smiling. *The Governor indeed has a secret.* And he shares it with his wife. It is of an intensely personal nature. There is no bitterness about it. They are together in their sadness; *together in a secret?*

He also deduces that the Governor, so concerned about time and schedule, who has arrived exactly one half hour before the bank opens, will be met by this same carriage at exactly one half hour past closing time.

I know his schedule.

The boy makes his way west, back toward Denmark Street and the apothecary shop. He can put in a full day of work and still get back here by half past four.

They are hiding something. I shall track them, and it!

6

THE GOVERNOR'S SECRET

There is a great deal to do at the apothecary shop these days, since the master's stamina has been failing so much. Lately, the old man has even taken to napping during business hours, very unlike him. But still, Sherlock can't bring himself to do all the cleaning, the tidying, the cataloguing of medicines and alkaloids that should be done this late morning and early afternoon. In fact, he spends a great deal of his time simply polishing the three statues of Hermes and staring off into the distance. Bell, trying to stifle his cough as always when his apprentice is around, doesn't mind this lack of industry, for he knows the boy's brain is finally engaged in something that fascinates him.

"I may not be home until late, very late," says the boy when he leaves. Bell merely nods with a smile. Sherlock runs when he gets outdoors. He must discover Stonefield's secret *soon*.

Despite starting out an hour beforehand, he still takes the short route to the City and the Bank of England. He goes north, follows Oxford Street east over the brand new Holborn Viaduct, then up the hill along Cheapside, and re-enters the financial district. The crowds are even thicker than this morning. It seems as if all of London's more than three million inhabitants are in the streets, a rush hour unparalleled on earth. As usual, the sounds almost deafen the ears, and talking on these busiest thoroughfares must be done in a shout. Though most every road is jammed with horses and vehicles, when he arrives at the bank just past four o'clock, still nearly half an hour before he anticipates the Governor will appear, the Bobbies have cleared a space in front of the entrance. The boy waits anxiously.

The carriage appears exactly on time, bearing, as Sherlock strains to confirm, Lady Stonefield. It is very curious, indeed – *a wife who rides to and from work with her husband.* He can see that her sad expression has not changed. And she remains in her mourning clothes. The great man comes out exactly on time and is led to his conveyance by burly lower bank officials, all young men who part the crowd without difficulty. Sir Ramsay's footman holds the door and nods to him. As Stonefield steps in and the footman takes his place, the carriage sags and creaks with their weight. Sherlock spies the Governor inside, taking his wife's hand as he shouts "Drive on!" The carriage slowly negotiates its way into the tight traffic.

Following them will not be difficult. The carriage will have to move at a crawl through London at this hour, and Sherlock will be able to keep it within sight. In fact, at times he actually has to wait for it, leaning against shop walls or canopy struts. It takes more than an hour to get back down Cheapside, along Oxford Street, and then south of the

British Museum and Irene's old Bloomsbury neighborhood. They pass north of the apothecary shop and continue west toward Soho. Sherlock is not surprised at where they seem to be heading. West is where the wealthy live. Soon they turn south on elegant Regent Street with its tall, curving buildings built with the shape of the road, and then west again into Mayfair.

Holmes has little reason to ever come to this wealthiest of London's neighborhoods, but it isn't just that that keeps him away. It was here, three years ago, that he found the Whitechapel murderer, and it was here that his mother was poisoned. He is thankful that today the carriage doesn't pass by the same streets, but comes to a halt in the north of the neighborhood at Hanover Square. A statue stands at the south end of a green park full of pigeons. It is beautified with a gorgeous garden in full bloom. Tall, stately homes, all imposingly Georgian in style and more than one hundred years old, line the square.

Sherlock stands in the park and stares at the scene, feeling insignificant. Sir Ramsay and Lady Stonefield are soon set down at the front of their beautiful five-storey mansion. *Now, I know where they live.* Their stone exterior has been painted purple. Big bay windows, twenty-four in total, run across every floor. A wrought-iron fence lines the frontage, which is just a step or so from the foot pavement. Stairs lead down to the servants' work area and a beautiful wide white set leads up to the impressive front door with a crescent window above it. The entrance opens and two liveried footmen come out to usher the owners inside. The couple hold hands, moving slowly, passing the four small Corinthian columns that support the stone awning on the porch, and enter. It is an unusual show of affection – many aristocratic couples barely see one another during a day, let alone deign to touch. Sherlock strains to look into the house's interior but can only glimpse the gleaming giant chandelier in the vestibule and the carved wooden staircase leading upward.

But he isn't particularly interested in the home's interior. No housebreaking for him this time, at least not yet. He has been training himself not to be impulsive, not to take chances before he must. All could be lost with a rash move. Besides, if the Governor and his wife have difficulties, something they want to hide, it is more than likely that it did not originate inside those doors. It is more apt to be some sort of business trouble of Sir Ramsay's. That is what Sherlock will investigate first – any unusual out-of-doors and after-hours movements on the Governor's part. The boy decides that he will stay here all evening, even into the night, and see if anyone suspicious comes to the door or if the Governor goes out. He hopes he will be in luck. He keeps thinking about Lady Stonefield's sad expression, her black clothing, the couple's constant attentiveness to one another.

He doesn't have to wait all night. Just before midnight, after all the lights have gone out in the house, a single groom brings one of the Governor's smallest carriages, a two-person, speedy hansom, from their stables to the front door. And then, out comes the Governor! He looks up and down the street and across into the park. Sherlock drops off his bench and under it. Then he hears the slight crack of the groom's whip and the horses moving away.

With that, Sherlock's plan is in ruins. There is almost no traffic in central London now, and the hansom is trotting out of Hanover Square at a good pace. The boy leaps to his feet and charges after it. But he knows that he cannot keep up for long. When it reaches Oxford Street, he sees a solution – but he will have to act quickly. He spots several cabs on the street, their horses munching in oat bags.

"Cab!" he cries.

In seconds, one has pulled up to him and he has offered all he has in his pocket – two shillings and sixpence – to the driver to follow the Governor's hansom without being detected. The man looks at him and hesitates, then looks at the coins and tells him to get in.

It turns out to be a long trip. They head south down beautiful Park Lane skirting the edge of Hyde Park, then turn west and drive through the wealthy neighborhoods of Knightsbridge and Kensington, and then along Hammersmith Road and out of the central London streets and into the suburbs. Sherlock keeps expecting them to stop. But the carriage continues to move. *Where could he be going at this late hour?* The road is nearly deserted. On past Chiswick they go, then into Kew where the serpentine River Thames curves up to meet the road. But they keep moving, all the way into the burgeoning village of Brentford.

The driver looks back.

"I can'ts go much further on those coins of yours, guv. Either we turn back soon, or you walk from wheres we land."

Sherlock nods for him to continue.

Several miles later, now a good ten or more from London, as they enter a place called Hounslow, the driver brings his cab to a halt on its High Street.

"That's it, sir. Either we turn 'round 'ere, or it's you on your pins back to London."

Sherlock leaps from the cab. *They can't be going much farther.* He runs with all he has after the carriage. It turns off High Street down a narrower road. He has to use his long legs to keep it in sight. Then it turns another corner onto an even smaller street. He loses sight of it. Desperate that his entire night's work will be for nothing but sure that the carriage, finding its way along narrow streets in Hounslow, must be nearing its destination, he puts his head back and sprints for the corner. But when he gets there, he stops dead in his tracks.

The carriage has pulled over. It is sitting on the side of a little residential street. He spots the driver still up in his position on the box, then looks ahead of the vehicle and sees the Governor walking alone, glancing around as if he is worried that he is being observed.

I cannot follow him. If I do, they will see me.

So, Sherlock doesn't turn onto the street the Governor has taken. Instead, he sprints even harder than before straight down the road he is on to the next corner, turns left there and races along that street until he comes to its first corner, turns left again and sprints up it until he finally comes to the end of the block. He has run three-quarters of a square and is now at the far end of the street that the Governor and his carriage are on. As Sherlock turns the corner, he sees Stonefield walking in his direction. Many of the two-storey homes here are row houses, connected to each other but a little better than working class, not broken down, and kept tidy and clean. Sherlock crouches behind a short hedge. Sir Ramsay stops at one of the houses! The boy had only seen him from behind when he alighted from his carriage. Observed from the front, it is evident that he is carrying a small bouquet of flowers. Way down the street, Sherlock can barely see the black carriage, still waiting on the side of the road.

The Governor of the Bank of England looks both ways. For an instant, his line of sight goes right toward Holmes. The boy ducks even lower. Stonefield turns back and quickly raps on the door with his walking stick: six knocks, three short and three long. The door opens and he goes in. Sherlock cannot see who has ushered him inside, but after a few seconds he stands up and closely observes the appearance of the home. It is much like the others though a little nicer, brightened up with a fresh coat of paint and decorated with an unusual number of flowers in small boxes. They are all red geraniums. The door is a mere three or four feet from the foot pavement, connected to it by a little walkway. He commits every detail to memory.

Half an hour later, the door opens again. Sherlock peeks around the hedge. The Governor is coming out. His head appears first as he looks both ways, up and down the street. Then he takes a step forward before turning to face someone in the doorway. Sherlock can see that it is a woman, a young woman, wearing a modest dress, though it is of a fashion that is slightly above her station. It is form-fitting and complete with a bustle on her behind. Sherlock Holmes, now sixteen, notices her lovely shape. Her pale skin and scarlet lips shine in the glow of the gaslights as she smiles.

The Governor of the Bank of England takes her into his arms!

Sherlock is so shocked that he stands up. The hedge is no more than a few feet high and he is clearly visible from the waist up. Stonefield turns in his direction. Holmes ducks down. He crouches there for a few moments, breathing heavily, praying that he has not been spotted. He counts to thirty and then peeks out. The Governor is calmly walking away, back up the street to his carriage in the distance.

He didn't see me.

Despite the fact that Sherlock has to walk twelve miles home to Denmark Street in London, he isn't upset, not in the least. He has something by the tail: a devil, or perhaps two. What he has seen may be the beginning of a trail that leads, somehow, to Grimsby. There is nothing in the world that he would rather do than bring down that little thug, and bringing him down may save not just one life but many more.

Blessed with Sigerson Bell's training in the arts of self-defense, the boy isn't distracted by the fear that he might be accosted on the way home. He knows how to steer clear of trouble, and if trouble comes his way, he can knock it down. And anyway, his horsewhip is tucked up his sleeve.

So, he has time to think clearly about what he saw. Three things are apparent to him by the time he reaches home just before dawn. The first was obvious the instant he saw the woman emerge from the house – he has seen the Governor's secret. The second is a little more complex and he spends more time considering its exact nature – it is likely that Malefactor knows this secret too; or is it just Grimsby? (Though the boy doubts the little one could mastermind this scheme himself.) And just before Sherlock gets to the shop, chewing on possibilities, a final idea begins to dominate his mind – if this is simply the case of the Governor being a bad boy, if this is solely *his* dirty secret, then why are both he and his wife, whom he seems to dearly love and genuinely have compassion for, always so sad, together?

It doesn't add up. He considers it again.

What if I could make it add up? What would it all mean then?

7

BAD MAN

The shop is silent when he wakes at nearly noon the following morning. Sigerson Bell, despite his poor health, is still going out to see patients these days.

"I have a man, a bricklayer in Lambeth," said the apothecary yesterday afternoon, explaining where he would be the following morning, "who swallowed a whistle whilst officiating at a local children's football match. He moves about the neighborhood whistling whenever he becomes excited and absolutely playing tunes when he is, uh, aroused, shall we say, by his lovely wife (and she is a most buxom woman, I might add) when she advances upon him in their marriage bed. She has insisted that I get it out or she does him grievous harm. It cannot be good for his digestive track either. I do not want to cut him open from stem to gudgeon, so I am developing a battle plan that may involve extricating said whistle from an aperture that is . . . not his mouth." The old man had raised his furry white eyebrows at Sherlock in a knowing look.

Thus, the shop is quiet. But when the boy finally gets out of his wardrobe and begins making his tea and heating a pair of the apothecary's legendary calf-brain scones, he keeps thinking he hears something. A bell always tinkles when the outer shop door opens and several times he stops to listen, wondering if it has gently jingled.

The coals are still hot in the fireplace. The boy stirs them, thinking of the note he left for Bell last night, telling him what he had been up to, what he had seen in Hounslow. He had done so because he knew the old man would appreciate it, love it, in fact. Sigerson Bell seems to thrive on intrigue and deeply enjoys the pursuit and destruction of evil. The two of them are well suited. He had asked his master to burn the note after he read it. He knew the old man would take joy in doing that too. It is nowhere to be seen.

But Sherlock continues to hear noises. He keeps making the trip from the laboratory into the outer room and the shop entrance, constantly thinking someone is either at it, or somewhere inside. Finally, he gives up and sits down at the lab table to eat. He drinks the tea, hot and black, as caffeine-filled as possible, and crouches over his scones. Something tells him to look up. When he does, someone is sitting across from him, staring into his eyes.

Malefactor!

Sherlock jumps to his feet and lets out a cry.

His enemy smiles at him. His top hat is resting on the lab table, gloves within it. "Master Sherlock Holmes, I perceive."

Holmes can't speak.

"You must construct a more complicated lock on your door, my boy. And you must develop some testicles. You look as though you have micturated into your trousers."

Sherlock looks down. He hasn't peed himself, but he might as well have.

"Malefactor," he says weakly, trying to slow his heartbeat.

"Ah, you recognize me. You are a genius."

The criminal does look different – older and his voice deeper. But that domed head, those sunken eyes, that way of extending his neck out as he speaks are all the same. He is dressed as a gentleman now, a black cravat tied perfectly under his starched white collar. His old black tailcoat is gone, replaced by a spotless new one of identical cut. Though he is just in his late teens, his hair is thinning on his pate.

"I have nothing to say to you," remarks Sherlock, "other than that your days in your despicable career are numbered. I may not have the wherewithal to pursue you fully now, but I can at least thwart your plans. When I have trained myself thoroughly, I will return, and destroy you."

"Such romantic words! But you have no grounds to do anything to me, sir, either now or in the future. You see, I am near to achieving the respectability I seek. I am well into my university training. Mathematics has seldom seen genius like mine. Chaos theory? The binomial theorem? They are child's play to me. I shall be esteemed within my world. On the surface, I will be as clean as the Queen's china. It shall be very difficult indeed to lay a hand upon a university professor of my standing."

"I will find a way."

"Higher education is in your future too, I hear."

How does he know that?

"I shall keep an eye on that skull of yours, Holmes, to see if it grows anymore. If it maintains its puny size, it will never contain what it must to confront the likes of me."

"We shall see."

"Take the occurrences of the last day or two, for example. You are making a poor job of it."

What does he know of my movements?

"Oh? How so?"

"Well, to confront Ronald Loveland in broad daylight. My God, have you learned nothing?"

"I was angry."

"Yes, you were undisciplined. You will not be a worthy enemy for me if you continue to do such things. It is rather disappointing."

"Here is something I do know. You follow people."

"Ah, you are not completely without a cranial sponge. Indeed, observing others closely is one of our prime operating principles. Yes, follow those of influence and learn little details that may be of use. But how did you know this? Never mind. It does not matter. I will someday be a man of enormous influence in this metropolis. In fact, I am approaching that position at a greater speed than even I predicted. The police are already not far from my grasp."

"Ronald Loveland will never ascend above his current station."

"Will he not?"

"I will see to it. In fact, I assure you that he shall soon lose the position he has now. I will keep his superior safe. I will stop any little plans you have."

"You will die first."

Sherlock pauses and tries to hide the fact that his heartbeat has instantly increased again. *Be calm. Learn something useful from him while he is in front of you.* Holmes speaks up.

"That is an idle threat. It does not concern me. And neither do you. I slept well last night, as I do every night, a good long sleep, not one thought of you. You, however, appear to have spent your night thinking of *me*, since you are here to confront me."

"On the contrary, Mr. Loveland simply mentioned that you were asking after my health, so I thought I should let you see that I am well and that you need not bother him anymore. I fear that it is *your* health that might take an immediate turn for the worse should you continue to worry yourself over his appointment. I slept like a baby last night, thank you for asking, though we *were* plotting."

Sherlock thinks for a moment before he responds.

"Plotting? In your lair?"

"As a matter of fact, yes, in my well-appointed country home, thank you very much, far from this rat-filled city. I shall never live here again. I will simply haunt it from afar. But I will never rest, especially when *anyone* is interfering with my plans."

"You may leave."

Malefactor looks startled. Holmes has abruptly dismissed him. Sherlock has discovered something during their conversation and now has no immediate use for his adversary.

I have what I need.

The criminal eyes Sherlock, examining his face, searching for what he has just been up to. Then he smiles. "Do not be too clever for your own good, my erstwhile friend."

"That is impossible."

"It would be a shame to lose you so early in the game." He gets to his feet. "And don't say I didn't warn you when you are lying in a pool of blood or gasping for breath. Leave the Treasury situation alone, and I will have no cause to harm you. I am and always shall be a gentleman, until I am pushed."

"You may see yourself out."

8

FAT MAN

Sherlock knows what his next move will be by the time Malefactor is back in the street. It is built upon two starting points. First, the information he has just cleverly gleaned from his opponent, without the villain detecting it: *"Malefactor said, 'WE were plotting.' And he said they were doing so in the countryside far from London. That means his lieutenants were with him last night discussing my confrontation with Grimsby, which also means that no one was following me. Malefactor didn't think I would act so quickly, acquire so much information so fast. He does not know that I have learned whose secret they are on to and exactly where that secret is housed on that street in Hounslow."* Sherlock is so excited that he is speaking out loud. He pauses for an instant to consider the second idea that is motivating his plans. But he doesn't get to it.

"Aha!" says a high-pitched voice from upstairs. Sherlock almost drops off his laboratory stool.

"Sir!" he screeches up at Sigerson Bell. "How long have you been up there?"

"Well," says the apothecary and begins to descend the spiral staircase. But he sees that it will be too slow a process, a painful one that he does not want the boy to observe. He doesn't have the appetite for another slide down the banister either, though the goose-down pillow is in its place at the bottom of the steps. So, he edges back up to the top and lies on his side, glowing down at his charge, excited to be playing detective again. "Well, I went out early this morning to see my whistling man in Lambeth. By the way, I was indeed able to extricate said whistle from his innards, out that passage that is decidedly NOT the mouth but located in the nether regions. To be more precise, I removed it from his ar –"

"Sir! I do not need that information. Just tell me how you came to be upstairs without my knowing it."

"Oh, yes, of course, my young knight. Let me see, I was coming home from my appointment when I spied Mr. Malefactor (though you and I know that is not his real name) crossing Trafalgar Square with that other lout of his, not Grimsby but the bigger one?"

"Crew?"

"Yes, Mr. Crew, a frightening individual, if I may say so. Something not quite normal in his upper stories. One can deduce as much by the look of him."

"Agreed."

"They appeared to be on the march and headed this way, so I followed them, surreptitiously and adroitly, since, as you know, I am skilled in such things."

"You are?"

"Sherlock, just go along with what I say, please! So, I skillfully followed them –"

"Because they never thought they'd be followed by

an old man who appeared incapable of doing anyone any real harm."

"Uh, yes, perhaps that is true, though that is an unkind interpretation and I would rather see myself as remarkably elusive and sensationally unpredictable."

"Understandable."

"And, what do you know, but they come right up Denmark Street, Crew beginning to lag behind a little and looking about. I could tell he was going to be the sentinel, the lookout for his leader, his, as the Germans say, *führer*. Malefactor was rummaging about in his coat."

"Looking for his lock-springing tool?"

"Yes, Master Holmes, indeed. Now, we come to a part of the story of which I am not particularly proud."

"Oh?"

"I have a secret entrance to the shop, the location of which I have kept from you." He drops his head, looking a little ashamed.

"A secret entrance?"

"Well, you didn't ask."

"Hmm."

"There were days, after the death of my lovely witch, when I was pursued most vigorously by many beautiful ladies intent upon locking me up into matrimonial entanglements. I was often in fear that they would tear the very clothes from my body."

"Really?"

"You sound surprised."

"Oh, no, sir."

"So, I needed a secret entrance. I have told no one of it until this moment, but I am telling you now so you may use it in the future. In fact, I have a feeling you may have need of it very soon."

"Soon?"

"Yes, but more of that in a moment. I quickly (well, maybe not so quickly) and inconspicuously (well, maybe not so inconspicuously) walked around to the rear of the shop, down the little lane not more than two feet wide at the back, entered the shop via my secret entrance, and made my way up to my bedroom via a dumb waiter I keep for such purposes in the wall. I was installed in a very quiet position by the time you finally noticed that Malefactor was in the laboratory. I saw his marvelous performance and your, at times, stirring response. My, there were moments when he made you look like a fool, a complete idiot, a nincompoop of the first order, a horse's –"

"Sir, you need not convey your thoughts on that subject in such rich, descriptive words."

"I suppose not."

"You heard everything?"

"Oh, yes, everything, even that last part that you spoke out loud to yourself. But I believe I cut you short. You had more to say, did you not?"

"Yes."

"So, your further plans are?"

Sherlock is reluctant to tell him. It is enough that the sickly old man was following Malefactor and the dangerous Crew through London to the shop. But then Sigerson Bell begins to cough. He retches for almost a minute, holding his handkerchief up to his mouth, hiding the liquid that he ejects into it. Sherlock moves toward the spiral staircase, looking up at his master. He wishes he could at least put a hand on his shoulder to comfort him. He had done so just a week or so ago during another coughing fit. Bell had felt alarmingly bony and his skin had been hot and wet through his shirt.

My master is dying. I love him. He is thrilled by what I am going to do with my life. He has always, in his own way, wanted to be part of it. He will be dead very soon.

"Sir, let me tell you what I am planning."

The old man stops coughing and looks down at Sherlock with a suddenly resplendent expression.

"You read my note about what transpired last night and you burned it, I believe?"

"Indeed!" Bell is veritably glowing, leaning slightly forward as if to urge more information out of his ward.

"As you heard, while I spoke out loud to myself, I am now sure that Malefactor is not aware that I suspect he knows Sir Ramsay Stonefield's secret. He and his closest associates were not on the streets of Hounslow last night."

"Yes, that was very clever, my young knight! You drew that out of him without his detecting it! Brilliant!"

"Thank you, sir, it was a trifle." Sherlock is surprised to feel his face glowing. "That information combined with an incomplete theory I have has hatched my next move."

"You are going back to Hounslow in the small hours of the morning!"

Sherlock pauses. Bell has done it again. He has veritably read the boy's thoughts, and not *just* his thoughts, but rather involved plans that he hadn't assumed the old man would follow. But this is not new.

"Yes. Yes, I am."

"My secret entrance will come into play concerning that, but go on."

"Something worried me about what I saw last night, and it had nothing to do with simply discovering that Stonefield has a secret. It is the fact that this secret is not exactly what it seems."

"Why do you say that?"

"Because they are both sad."

"They?"

"Sir Ramsay *and* his wife. I do not think that this secret is just his. I think it is somehow *theirs,* together."

"So, that is why you must go back!"

"Precisely. This is not a matter of simply being aware that Malefactor knows Stonefield has a woman on the side. If it were so, then my only task would be to, first, bring Grimsby down, and then perhaps to expose the Governor as a cad."

"Oh, you wouldn't do that. None of your business, sir! Gentleman must be allowed such things."

"I'm not sure I agree, but nevertheless, he may not be such a cad after all. I must go back and find out just *exactly* what this is about. That and that alone will lead me to what I will do next. It is the key to everything I must undertake."

"And so, I give you my secret entrance! You must use it. You cannot go out our front door. You must slip out the back!"

"That is an excellent suggestion, sir, but not enough."

"Not enough?"

"I must be in disguise as well. Who knows what sort of surveillance Malefactor has in place. He is desperate to protect Grimsby's position at the Treasury, anxious to push him forward very soon. He will want to know *exactly* what I know. Going out a back entrance will help, but if I go out as myself, someone will see me in the streets before too long. The very letterboxes will be watching."

"You could go dressed as Sigerson Bell again!"

"We must not repeat ourselves."

"Then what?"

"You have an unusual array of clothing, sir."

Sigerson Bell has been known to dress in some of the strangest apparel in London, and that is saying something. A red fez, a green greatcoat, a pink Egyptian robe, loincloths, fighting leotards, and some of the most colorful nightshirts on the earth hang in his wardrobe. Or lie in piles at the bottom of it.

"I do?"

"Let us take a look at *all* of them."

Moments later, the old man is throwing every spot of clothing he owns down the spiral staircase toward the boy. It is indeed a remarkable collection. Not only do the spectacular nightshirts, fezes, greatcoats, leotards, and robes descend, but there are many items that look to have been featured in costume balls, including crowns, furs, and a few dresses (the boy doesn't ask). But one item, which billows in the air and takes a long time getting to the bottom of the stairs, catches Sherlock's eye.

"What is this?" he asks, holding the massive piece of material up to the old man, who slides his face over and peers down from above.

"Just the Fat Man's trousers," he says and yawns.

"A fat man?"

"No, no, no, not *a* fat man, *the* Fat Man. Oberon Obese, they called him. He weighed more than fifty stone in his heyday. That is rather large, my boy. He came to me in retirement, asking to shed some flesh. I managed, through skillful control of his diet and a regimen of exercise, to cut him in half, down to a svelte, how would your generation put it, 350 or so pounds? He gave me his trousers as a souvenir."

"And you kept them?"

"Of course! Why not?"

"Yes." Sherlock smiles. "Why not?" He looks up at his master. "I have an idea."

9

A DEEPER SECRET

Sherlock Holmes doesn't attend Snowfields School every day any more. There is little that they can teach him now. He has had the best grades in this working-class institution near the London Bridge Railway Station since the day he entered it and lately has been applying himself like an addict in an East London den to his opium. He has been a pupil-teacher for two years and has been urged to take his papers to become a full-fledged teacher. His headmaster assures him that he could someday helm the school. But Holmes has informed him that he has other, undisclosed ambitions that involve his attending one of England's best universities. Though the headmaster has come to admire Sherlock Holmes a great deal, he wonders how a half-Jew in a lowly school, however brilliant, can even consider the idea of being an Oxford or Cambridge man. Both schools have only recently allowed Jews admission, and the poor, of course, never attend. But not wanting to discourage his prize pupil, the master is tutoring him in advanced subjects required at the great schools. This is being given twice a week in exchange for three days of Holmes's own tutoring of Snowfields' most accomplished students.

Sherlock is scheduled to be at school the morning after Malefactor's appearance in the shop. His enemy will know if he does not attend. Crew or others (or perhaps the letter-boxes) will not only be watching the shop's front door, but all of Denmark Street, the adjoining arteries, and probably the boy's entire route to Snowfields.

Just before six o'clock that morning, a good three hours before school begins, an enormously fat man emerges from the apothecary shop's secret rear entrance, after sliding back the long painting of Hermes that hangs low on a wall of the laboratory. The gargantuan chap then edges along the narrow lane at the back of the building and moments later plods out onto Denmark Street from the alleyway five doors down. He is wearing a big floppy felt hat that looks like something a swashbuckling French musketeer might sport. It hangs down over his face, which is also obscured by long, strangely thick, black and white hair. He wears a coat so huge that it looks like two stitched together, and inside his bloated trousers is one of England's most spectacular bellies, a shelf-like protrusion that extends a good three feet out at his middle, leading him this way and that as he waddles along. He turns north on Denmark, not south, heads up to Oxford Street, and then hails a cab. The first few will not take him, their drivers noticing his girth and perhaps taking pity upon their horses, but finally one allows him in and the vehicle sags like a deflated balloon and pulls away, westward, toward Hammersmith, Chiswick, and Hounslow.

But magically, the hansom cab has *two* passengers by the time it reaches the far end of Hyde Park, and drops one of them there, a very thin one. He is an old man in the shape of a question mark and he is carrying a huge coat and gigantic trousers. He slowly strolls south toward Whitehall, leaving a sixteen-year-old boy in the cab to travel all the way to Hounslow.

Inside the carriage, Sherlock grins at his plan. When the boy had seen Oberon Obese's extraordinary trousers, an outlandish idea had come to him. He had considered how slight and light Bell had become and how his own height – he now towers over Bell – and the master's unique shape might be put together in the guise of a single remarkable man. He then devised a scheme in which the apothecary's forehead would be placed against his own midsection, the old feet on top of the young ones, and the rest of Bell's withering little frame put inside those huge trousers with him and under two coats stitched together. Horse-tail hair (a key apothecary's medicinal ingredient) was used for human locks under the hat.

Within an hour, Holmes is on High Street in Hounslow. No one is following him. He must get back to the apothecary shop and then on to school without being detected. It has to seem, to anyone who might be observing, that today is a normal day for him. Bell has given him enough money to get to the far suburbs and back. They have agreed to meet near Hyde Park Corner at about the time Big Ben strikes eight and slip into the trees there to re-costume themselves as the Fat Man. Simply wearing padding underneath the big trousers was not an option – a mighty amount would have been needed to give Sherlock the girth he wanted and everything would have to have been stashed before he went to Hounslow *and* still be available when he returned. As well, he could not secretly watch the house as a huge Fat Man; he would have stuck out like the proverbial sore thumb in the suburbs. Neither would he have been able to effectively run away in such a disguise. And with Bell (magically) out of the shop and unobserved as such, the old man could spend his time near the Treasury, making sure that Grimsby was still going to work.

Sherlock instructs the driver to turn off High Street at exactly the spot where Sir Ramsay's carriage turned the other night, but stops him before he gets to the narrow road where the house sits. He asks him to wait there. The boy gets out, turns onto the little street, and cautiously makes his way along it until he comes to the front of the residence.

The house looks quiet. Sherlock is guessing that it is nearing seven o'clock. It is likely that this "kept" woman has no occupation outside her home, but Sherlock is figuring she does *something* on her front step or beyond in the morning, even if she simply emerges to water her many flowers or goes out of doors to take the air. He desperately hopes that this is a perfect time for her to appear, otherwise this daring outing is for nothing. He needs to observe her again in the hope that doing so will help him unravel the exact nature of this secret. But he doesn't have much time, hardly any at all.

After another ten or fifteen minutes of nothing stirring at the house, the boy, who is by turns hiding behind the hedge he used the other night and strolling back and forth along the street, decides to do something he knows is very risky. He thinks of the danger Grimsby's superior may be in. *I have to learn something, anything.*

He walks past the house and stops right on the front walkway. He glances through the little front window and cannot see any movement inside. He looks down, but at first can't make out any markings on the brick walkway, which is covered with a thin film of dirt. *At least it hasn't been thoroughly swept.* Sherlock knows he shouldn't, but he drops down anyway, onto his knees on the bricks. He examines them closely. *There!* He sees shoe prints. But there are several: faint ones from well-made, expensive footwear, and others, more clearly marked, from a gentleman of more modest means. He spots lady's prints too, and lines, as if made by narrow wheels. He had thought that such indicators on the walkway might tell him something. But they have made things even more mysterious.

At that instant he hears voices approaching the door from the inside. He leaps to his feet, dusts off his knees, and begins to walk away as quickly and yet as inconspicuously as possible. He can hear the door open sharply behind him. He crosses the street, moving fast. Then, he realizes something.

I won't be able to see her!

So, he takes another chance. Once he is twenty or so strides down the narrow foot pavement on the other side of the street, he turns around and walks back. He is praying that she is preoccupied with whatever she is doing, perhaps watering those flowers, did not see him striding away, and thus won't be suspicious of his coming back. He looks toward the house as he passes. What he sees shocks him.

The person who has just come out the door isn't the woman. It is a man. *Thirty-five years old, reasonably handsome, square jaw, dark hair, suit not particularly well tailored, short top hat, bag and meal in hand for a short journey: a clerk of some sort, off to London.* The man has his back to Sherlock and seems to be struggling with something. The boy gets nearer the house. That's when he realizes that the man isn't struggling; he is embracing and kissing a woman rather passionately. And that woman, though now more modestly dressed, is without a doubt the *same* woman Sherlock saw the night before last in the arms of the Governor of the Bank of England!

The boy has to stop himself from gaping. He moves on and comes to the end of the street and ducks down behind the hedge again. He looks back at the house. The man is departing in the other direction toward High Street where a Great Western Railway Station moves daytime passengers to and from London. The man turns and gives the woman a wave. She blows him a loud kiss, sending it flying down the street.

What is this about? The footprints in the walkway from the less expensive set of shoes were all identical and more numerous than the Governor's. If they belong to this chap, then he has been in and out of the house several times over the last night or two. Perhaps he was even in there the very night Sir Ramsay was here! But who is he? And WHAT is she? Does she entertain men in the early hours in her home? Is she a prostitute? Was the Governor merely one of her clients, just like this man? But did this one stay all night? And why did his affection for the woman bear all the hallmarks of a husband's tender love? But the Governor embraced her with great affection too. Is this man sharing his wife and her favors? London and its environs contain much evil, Sherlock knows that. But this is something new again!

He cannot stand there thinking. He must be on his way. If he doesn't leave in moments, he will be late for his meeting with Bell and they will not be back at the shop in time for him to get away to school on schedule. It is imperative to keep any followers off his Hounslow trail. But just as he steps out from the hedge to walk down the street toward his carriage, the door of the house opens again. He ducks back down.

The woman is coming out. She is indeed a beautiful lady, even when dressed in this modest outfit. Her auburn hair is pinned up under a blue bonnet that matches her dress. She has the face of an angel. *Can this woman be a dabbler in extramarital games?* And what she is pushing in front of her seems to bring that idea even further into question. She is steering a wheelchair along the walkway and out onto the foot pavement. In it sits a woman or a girl – it is difficult to tell from Sherlock's vantage point. The invalid is wearing a dark dress and her face is covered with a veil. *It is a hot day*, thinks Holmes. *Perhaps that is why.*

But the boy can't look any closer. The woman and her companion are coming directly toward him! He slides away and strides around the block. As he does, he notices a park about a cannon shot in the distance at the far end of this residential area. The woman seems to be heading toward it. Sherlock moves on, as fast as he can go without drawing attention. He runs to his cab and instructs the driver to head to the city at double speed.

He has a great deal to tell the apothecary, but no idea what it all means.

10

BEHIND THE VEIL

Though Bell is thrilled by this latest Hounslow story, he too is unable to make sense of it.

The following day is a Friday, and the boy goes back to school. Though it scares him to take a day off from his pursuit of the Governor's secret – time may be running out – he thinks it best not to return to that suburban street right away. As well, he must have more time there during his next visit. In the morning, he sends a note round to Mycroft, asking him if all is well at the Treasury. He is relieved to receive a message back that evening with the following words: *Interesting question; all is tranquil.* Grimsby's superior must still be at his desk, neither dead nor missing.

Holmes is ready when Saturday dawns. He will have the whole day to himself. He must strike now; he must go back to the suburbs and discover more while he can; he must take whatever chances are necessary. The Fat Man ruse may not work many more times.

He knows that the best course is to arrive at precisely the same hour as last time. The English are creatures of habit – witness the Governor's tight schedule at the Bank of

England. Sherlock is guessing that the woman, whether the man is there or not, and whether he travels to work on a Saturday or not, will go out with the person in the wheelchair at about the same time. It must be their routine to take the air at that hour.

He is also guessing that they will walk to that park. So, he wears different clothes under the Fat Man costume this morning, the paraphernalia of a dustman.

Bell and Holmes execute their shop escape perfectly again, and Sherlock arrives at the little Hounslow street on time. The woman comes out when expected with the wheelchair and her companion. The man does not appear. Without waiting for them to pass by, the boy quickly makes his way to the park ahead of them. He has brought a broom, a dustpan, and a sack, all easily concealed in the Fat Man costume, and is hard at work cleaning the park when the other two arrive. Trusting that they didn't see him on his last visit and in his ability to play his part, he plans to get very close to them.

The park is rectangular in shape and not very big, about one-quarter the size of a football pitch. A rather clumsy statue of the Duke of Wellington sits in the middle, with six gravel footpaths leading to it like spokes in a wheel. Sherlock heads toward the center to gain the best vantage point in the park. Six black wrought-iron benches with wooden seats face the statue and six more are stationed looking toward the lawns between the footpaths. Each of those lawns is decorated with a bed of flowers.

The person in the wheelchair is confined to it and only goes out of doors briefly. So, where will they go first? She will be taken to see the flowers. Which ones? What are the probabilities? Likely, the most beautiful bed before the others. She won't want to wait, and the woman pushing her, having to contend with an invalid's frustration over being confined to a chair, won't deny her, will want her happy immediately. I must be there before they arrive. I cannot appear to be seeking them out in any way.

Sherlock quickly evaluates the flowers. Each bed seems to be the same size and features the same blossoming brilliance of colors in this mid-June morning.

Which one? He thinks back to what he knows of the people in that home, the little he knows. He pictures the exterior of their house, summoning a clear photograph in his mind. . . . *Geraniums! That's what they have in their flower boxes. They must be the favorite of someone in that house. Dickens loved red ones. They have been mentioning it in the papers. It is in the news. There is a high probability that they will look for geraniums.*

Sherlock surveys the park and finds a bed bursting with blood-red geraniums. He begins to walk slowly down a footpath toward the bench closest to it. His shoes crunch on the gravel. He smells the sweet fragrance of the flowers on this dewy English morning and heads out onto the grass behind the bench. He assumes the wheelchair will be positioned right near here, directly in front of these beauties.

Though he doesn't look up, he uses his peripheral vision to see that the woman pushing the chair comes to a sudden halt when she enters the park and notices his presence. For a moment, he wonders if she will turn back to the house.

No!

But she moves forward.

That was curious. Why did she hesitate? She noticed me. It is as if she doesn't want to be in the park when anyone else is in it. Is that why they always come early? But she must have decided that a mere dustman wasn't of concern. Is she ashamed of being with the one in the wheelchair? And if so, why?

He keeps his distance, eyes on the ground, searching out rubbish littered on the grass. He finds the butt of a cigar, an empty bottle of tincture of opium, and the broken-off cover of a book, and sweeps them all into his dustpan and drops them into his sack. As he does, he glances toward the other two. The woman pushing the chair is keeping her eye on him as well. But she brings the invalid up the exact footpath that Holmes suspected she would follow. She turns the chair toward the geraniums, lowers her head to the veiled face and speaks to her in a low voice, sounding kind and caring.

What are they saying?

He wants to know. But he dare not get closer. Then the woman does something that changes his mind. She reaches down and pulls the veil from the other one's face. Sherlock is still behind them.

I must see her.

He moves toward them, walking much faster than before. The woman seems alarmed and quickly drops the veil back over the invalid. Sherlock is so close that he can hear the seated one's voice. It sounds muffled, as if she were bound with a gag in her mouth. The woman leans down and speaks quietly to her again, even quieter than before, almost in a whisper.

What is this about?

The woman turns to him and catches his eye as he looks back.

Mistake.

The time has come to do something rash, very rash. They are wary of him and may be about to leave. If they do, he will have nothing. He cannot even go back to the house and examine it. This woman has looked directly into his face, and despite it being smeared with a dustman's dirt, he doubts she would have trouble recognizing him again. She would be suspicious if he came near her house dressed as he is, and even more so if he dressed differently. This may also be the last day he can come here. What are the chances that he can elude Malefactor again?

I must take a chance. Now.

A bee buzzes past. Sherlock Holmes loves bees. He isn't sure why – perhaps because they are misunderstood. Everyone fears them. He loves that too. *But they do so much for us, for nature.* He admires their systematic way of living, their delineation of male and female duties, their perfect design, and their brilliant yellow and black clothing, everything so attractively in order.

The bee nears the wheelchair, heading toward the flowerbed.

One can always find a way to solve a problem. Use what you have at your command. Take stock of what you possess: any items at hand, no matter what they are. What does my dustman's equipment allow me to do?

He looks down at the broom, hears the bee buzzing near, and something comes to him.

Sigerson Bell likes to teach his lad many different ways to defend himself. Though he has shown him the mysterious ways of Bellitsu, pugilism, and deft wrestling maneuvers, he sometimes surprises his charge with demonstrations of even stranger fighting resources.

"One must have a myriad of weapons at one's fingertips," the old man likes to say. "One must also not be afraid to inflict pain upon others who deserve it! Should you pursue this reckless crime-fighting ambition you have – and a fine one it is – you must enter into it armed like an Oriental ninja!"

The boy smiles as he remembers the war whoop Bell let out the day he told him that. The apothecary was standing in the laboratory, dressed in his leotards and the other startling pieces of his fighting costume, stripped to the waist of course, bent over, flesh hanging down like doughy stalactites, but a glint in his eye.

"Swordsmanship is a worthy addition to the Bellitsu and pugilistic skills I have instilled in you! And romantics like myself excel at it!"

With that, he had produced a sword from the fighting colors around his waist (given to him by the great pugilist Tom Sayers, "The Napoleon of the Prize Ring") and brandished it in the boy's face, inches from his nose.

"Sir!" Sherlock had cried, "for goodness sake, be careful."

"A little too close-quartered for you, my young steed?" Bell had replied. "One must operate with precision at all times!" He then turned and sliced off the skull of one of the human skeletons that Sherlock had nailed to the wall the previous day. (The apothecary was notorious for destroying his bony corpses in displays of fighting prowess.) "But!" exclaimed the old man, dropping the sword to the floor. "But! But! But!" He whirled around and suddenly two long sticks, thick and round and as hard as steel, were in his hands. They were each about five feet long.

The broom in Sherlock's hands this day in the suburban park is exactly that length.

"These, my young mercenary of justice," Bell had continued, "are what we in the dark arts know as Swiss Fighting Sticks!"

"Dark arts?" the boy had queried.

"Sherlock, stay with me! Do not question the adornments, the flourishes I may add to my descriptions. Fiction contains the greatest truths!"

Holmes had had no idea what the old man meant by that, but he kept quiet. Bell began slamming the sticks together, wielding them in all sorts of ways and directions, and then pivoted and swung them toward a shelf filled with glass bottles. "Pin-point accuracy is the hallmark of the use of Swiss Fighting Sticks. One must be able to swing at something and hit it upon the nose! Or miss by a quarter of an inch!" But then Bell swung at the bottles, a mighty swoop that cut the air with the sound of a bullwhip and would have killed a rhinoceros had it been standing in the shop (and the boy wouldn't have been surprised to see one, one day) and hit the glass containers dead in their centers, sending them, and the shelf, crashing to the floor with the sound of two locomotives colliding.

It took several seconds for the sound to subside. The old man had stood there staring at what he had done for almost a full minute. The boy had not dared to utter a word.

"Well . . ." Bell finally said, looking sheepish, "one sometimes misses!"

But the apothecary then taught the boy to never miss. At first, he was shown how to use the Fighting Sticks to knock a lemon-flavored sweet from the old man's mouth from a distance of five feet, and had several times loosened Bell's teeth. But within a month the entire art had been added to his repertoire. Sherlock Holmes could swipe a pea from the top of the apothecary's balding head . . . while wearing a blindfold.

The bee buzzes near the invalid's veiled face. The young dustman steps forward, lifts his broom in a decidedly martial-art grip, hands exactly six inches apart, the business end of the weapon pointed directly at his target, and swings his weapon at the bee, sweeping both it and the invalid's veil across the footpath and thirty feet toward the flowerbed. The end of the broom, of course, does not touch the girl's face, but passes a tiny fraction of an inch from her right cheekbone and her nose, lifting the veil away as cleanly as if he had delicately done it with a feather touch of his fingers.

The woman behind the wheelchair screams.

And when Sherlock Holmes looks at the face staring out at him from that chair, he nearly does too.

11

EVIL INCARNATE

Sitting before him is a monster. Or, at least, it is the face of a monster atop the body of a teenage girl. His father never allowed him to attend circuses and see the freaks in the sideshows, and since Sherlock left home he has never once succumbed to the temptation to visit the penny gaffes on Whitechapel Road in the East End where strange people are exhibited in back rooms, often presented as part elephant or crossbred with some other exotic animal.

"They are suffering from diseases, my boy!" Sigerson Bell once proclaimed. "We are not to gawk at them as if they were creatures from the Dark Continent."

But the boy cannot help but "gawk" at this person, with a head twice the normal size, hideous growths ballooning from her forehead, skin like a crocodile's, lips puffed and bloated, all framed with beautiful blonde hair, as blonde and glowing as Irene Doyle's. Sherlock looks into the monster's eyes. They stare back, blue like the June sky, filled with curiosity.

"You beast!!" cries the woman, rushing to pick up the veil.

But the boy cannot respond. He cannot offer his excuse: that he had been merely swatting at the bee, protecting the girl in the chair. Repulsed by the horrible face, standing there almost catatonic with shock, his eyes remain locked on her eyes, which now begin to smile back.

The woman retrieves the veil and knocks into the boy with a thump as she rushes past him. Then she snatches the disguise over the girl's face again, screams at Sherlock once more, and wheels her charge away. They march back toward their street.

Sixteen or seventeen years old; right arm and leg horribly deformed too; left leg incapable of movement. She is –

But he can't go on. He can't analyze this person. He doesn't have the heart. He pities her from the bottom of his soul. The deformities sear into his memory as he remains rigid, standing in exactly the same position he was in the instant the veil came off. That face will wake him up at nights. It is a complicated reaction. He sees those eyes too – their curiosity and their smile.

He shakes himself from his haze and turns back toward the street. *I must apologize.*

There is no sign of them, either here or in the distance. As he stumbles out of the park, he realizes that he must have been standing there for a very long time. He wonders what, in God's name, he can say to them. *I must tell them the truth. They need to know why I was here. They deserve to hear it. I must come clean.*

When he first sees the house, the door is closed and all appears quiet. But as he reaches the walkway, he hears voices.

They are raised. One belongs to the woman and the other seems familiar. He moves closer.

Grimsby!

"How did you get in here?" He hears the woman cry. "Who are you?"

Grimsby's long response is muffled. Sherlock can only hear parts of it.

He must have been waiting for them at their door! The other man, this woman's man, obviously isn't here. *He must have gone out while we were in the park.* Did Grimsby know he would be away at this hour? He has the woman all alone in there and is beginning to shout at her. *Grimsby isn't just a villain; he's a coward too!* Sherlock had been trying to summon the courage to knock on the door but now he bursts in.

"I shall be wanting two bob a week for meself!"

"But I can't pay you that! We can't afford that!"

The detective in Sherlock stops him just inside the door. The other two are yelling so loudly now that they don't hear him enter. He is in a tiny vestibule, a few out-of-doors clothes hanging on hooks in an open closet to his right and a narrow wall blocking the next room, the parlor, from view. Grimsby and the woman are in there, embroiled in their argument, unaware of his presence.

You must listen. Learn. This might unlock everything.

"Ask Stonefield for the money, woman."

"He won't give it to me."

"Yes, 'e will. You keep 'is secret; 'e is much obliged to you. I knows 'uman nature and I knows folks pays for what they must 'ave, for what they wants. Just asks 'im for a raise in what 'e pays you."

"I will not! I will expose you! Blackmailer! I will notify the police!"

"You ain't listening, is you? I told you, your guvna' 'e don't want this 'ere situation to get out, so 'e pays me boss what 'e must." Then Grimsby's voice drops, almost as if he is talking to himself. "Me boss sent Crew 'ere yesterday and I followed 'im I did, on the quiet. Taught well, I was." His voice rises again. "So, now I knows."

Yesterday, thinks Sherlock. *The only day I didn't come here. Crew was sent to see if I was on the trail. What would he have done if he'd found me?*

"Sir Ramsay pays the man you work for?" says the woman. "Some scoundrel?"

"It's not in coins."

"Then, in what?"

"Never you mind in what. I wants two quid from you and your 'usband, starting Monday next. Or I tells *The News of the World.* No more questions."

Husband. That man is her husband.

"But I can't ask Sir Ramsay. He has been through so much. He and the Missus! Have pity!"

"Pity on the rich? Me?" Grimsby lets out a horrible giggle.

"He loves her. He loved the other one too!"

Loves her? The other one too?

"I ain't 'ere on a mission of charity or to 'ear the sob stories of the privileged. Now you do as you is told or your master's secret will be public knowledge."

"Leave this house immediately!"

Sherlock hears a struggle and the woman begins to scream. He also hears a garbled sound, the pitiable cry of a teenage girl, terrified but wordless.

Holmes springs into action. He darts out of the vestibule and into the parlor. He sees the woman and Grimsby grappling with each other. He attacks the rascal from behind, gripping him in a lock that drives his forearms down and against his hips, and pulls him away from woman, releasing her. But Sherlock doesn't stop at that. He is incensed. Locking Grimsby so tightly that he almost cracks his ribs, he effects a Bellitsu move, placing his right foot in front of his opponent's, twisting him violently and sending him sailing backward over his own upper thigh and hips. The startled little man lets out a cry as he crashes down onto his head and shoulders in the parlor and rolls all the way into the tiny back kitchen. Holmes is at him in a flash. Grimsby leaps to his feet, his little hands balled in fists. The woman lets out a scream. As Sherlock nears his enemy, he sees that the girl in the wheelchair is right there, inches from the blackguard, near the top of the stairs to the cellar. Holmes wants to kill him now; failing that, he wants to maim him for life. A hatred for Grimsby and Malefactor and for the man who killed his mother and for everyone who brings evil and hatred and injustice into the world rises up in him. He hates the fact that the poor girl sits in that wheelchair, disfigured and crippled. His eyes are on fire, the veins pop out on his neck and forehead, and he flushes red. *The time has come.*

But the girl in the chair is in his line of vision, behind

Grimsby. Her veil is off and she holds her hands in front of herself in shame, terrified, sobbing, her shoulders heaving. Those blue eyes peek out from between her fingers, catching sight of Sherlock. When their eyes meet, hers turn hopeful.

He cannot hurt anyone in her presence, not even this devil. The woman sees Sherlock clearly now.

"Why, you're the dustman!" she says.

But Holmes is glaring at Grimsby.

"Villain!" he cries.

"'Ow did you find this place 'olmes? You is an arse, but you ain't without wits. I –"

"Out from here, you wretch! Now!"

"It won't matter. I will return!"

"Not on my watch!"

"You can't make me, 'olmes."

"No, but Malefactor can."

Grimsby goes silent. Sherlock grins.

"He won't like this, will he? He doesn't know you are here. This is just your scam, isn't it, you thug. Thought you'd shave a little more off the top without his knowledge, did you?"

"What do I gain from working in the Treasury? It's not enough."

"Can't wait for the rewards, can you?"

"They're mostly 'is."

"You thought you could do this without anyone knowing, didn't you? This is a tissue of lies and secrets. You thought you'd add one more and, because these folks don't know what is *really* going on, you'd be safe."

"I is."

"Not now."

"You wouldn't tell 'im."

"I would!"

"But 'e's your enemy, 'olmes!"

"Enemies can be used, especially to destroy other fiends!"

The woman steps forward, taking the veil from the kitchen table, about to put it over the young one's face. "What are you two talking about? This poor girl is none of your business! You must leave! Both of you!" The invalid in the wheelchair is smiling up at Holmes.

"You put his enterprise in danger, Grimsby," says Sherlock, ignoring the woman. "When I tell him, he will be VERY angry."

Grimsby's face looks as if it might explode. His hatred for Sherlock Holmes rises within him. He stands there boiling, thinking about how his master opposes the brilliant half-Jew but somehow still respects him, much more than he respects his own lieutenant. Now, the half-breed is threatening to destroy even his opportunity at the Treasury, his chance of being someone special in Malefactor's eyes, not to mention his own little blackmailing scheme.

"I 'ate you, Sherlock 'olmes!" he cries. He turns and sees the cripple. Tears burst from his eyes like water released from a dam. "Useless freak!" he cries. It is hard to know if he means her or himself, but as he speaks he rears back and kicks the wheelchair as hard as he can. It tips over and falls with a crash to the top of the cellar stairs, and keeps rolling from the force of Grimsby's blow, rocking over onto the first step, and picking up momentum as it descends, thudding and slamming with great violence down the stairs, landing on its side, then its wheels, and then, at the bottom . . . on the invalid's huge, deformed skull. The woman shrieks. "Angela!!!" She runs to the top step. Sherlock and Grimsby stand where they are, their mouths wide open. The girl has landed on the hard cellar floor, and blood is running from her ears. Her neck is twisted at a grotesque angle. She isn't breathing.

The woman flies down to her. "Angela? Angela!!"

The girl's blue eyes are wide open. They stare up at Sherlock Holmes, unblinking and still.

"She's DEAD!" cries the woman, gasping and bringing her hands to her mouth.

Grimsby runs. In an instant he is out the door and down the street. Holmes wants to pursue him, tear him limb from limb. Their street fights were one-sided at first, but became closer affairs, and Holmes, with another year of lethal Bellitsu behind him, knows what he can do now. He can do the little one grievous harm.

But Sherlock can't run away. Not from this house. They need him. He forces his rubbery legs to move down the stairs. The woman turns, spits in his face and shoves him away.

"I was trying . . . to help," he pleads.

"You *killed* her, you and that little beast! Our beauty is dead! Just like Gabriella! What will Sir Ramsay say? It will break him!"

What will Lady Stonefield say? Will this break her too?

Sherlock wipes the spittle from his face.

The woman sobs for a while and he kneels near them, feeling helpless. "I am . . . sorry," she finally says to him through her tears. "It wasn't you. You *were* trying to help. It was that other little man, that horrible one." She sobs again. "I am sorry." She holds the big, broken head in her arms, the blood running onto her sleeve. "Oh, so sorry."

Sherlock can't believe that in her terrible grief she is able to take back her angry words, that she has concern for him. She is a good person, indeed.

He ascends the stairs. There is nothing else he can do here. His target is out there, running away.

After him!

"Who are you, really?" asks the woman.

Sherlock looks down at her. "A friend," he says quietly. Then he tears out the door.

But out on the street there is no sign of the criminal, not even in the distance. Holmes races to his hansom cab. It is gone. Grimsby has bribed the driver. Sherlock will never catch him.

He must walk back to London.

But then he hears something behind him. The woman has come running in his direction. She stands a hundred feet away on the foot pavement down the street and cries out, "Don't tell anyone! Do *not* try to bring him to justice! You can't!" She turns and rushes back to the house.

But Holmes is barely listening. He walks the first half of his journey in tears, and the last in growing anger, from red to white hot.

There are places I can search to find that rat. It is Saturday. He won't be at the Treasury. He will hide during the day.

But Sherlock is too distraught to go anywhere other than home. Because today was perhaps his last chance to go to Hounslow without being detected, he hadn't arranged to meet Bell and get back into their Fat Man costume. He had intended to go straight back to the apothecary shop in the dustman's clothes. So he does, but with absolutely no concern for being spotted. He doesn't care anymore.

It isn't his intention to tell Bell what he witnessed, but the moment he enters the shop, he scurries to the laboratory and pours his heart out to the old man.

"Go to the police. Tell your young Lestrade friend. They can be in Hounslow at a moment's notice. Both you and the woman are witnesses, and the crime scene is fresh!"

"I cannot do that."

"You what?"

"There are dark secrets there. The Governor wants them to stay hidden. That woman came all the way down the street to insist that I not tell anyone."

"But why?"

"I don't know."

Normally, Sherlock Holmes would have been hot on this trail, consumed with not only passion but curiosity. Nothing fascinates him more than a puzzle, a real and living puzzle, and this one matters deeply. But he is heartbroken.

He wonders if he can ever summon the energy again to be the crime fighter he wants to be. On top of everything, it seems to him that, once again, he has been the cause of a terrible tragedy. If he had not gone into that house and confronted Grimsby, that poor girl would still be alive.

He says nothing else to Bell and goes to bed. The old man senses his pain and wants to embrace him. But that sort of thing has never been a part of their friendship.

Sherlock lies in bed in his wardrobe and tosses and turns. He can't get the girl's blue eyes out of his mind: blue like his mother's and kind like Beatrice's, her blonde hair the very glowing image of Irene's, all on a hideous face. His anger at Grimsby and Malefactor and Crew grows. Finally, he gets to his feet and goes out into the dangerous London night, seething.

12

EVERYONE SINS

He wakes in a sweat and cries out. He can barely remember what he did last night, running through the darkest streets of London. He doesn't want to remember. He had returned with his head and heart pounding, stripped off his clothes, poured a cold bath in Bell's big tub in the lab, and washed himself over and over before finally crawling to his bed and, still naked, falling into a deep sleep.

But now, he tells himself, he must move forward. *What matters is what is before me, not behind. There are things I need to do.*

He decides upon a bold move. There is no time to waste. He will go directly to Stonefield and speak to him. He *must* know *exactly* what Sir Ramsay's secret is. The things he heard during that traumatic scene in the house in Hounslow paint a picture of what the Governor is hiding, but one without details. He remembers the woman calling Grimsby a "blackmailer" and the scoundrel replying that his boss was being paid but "not in coins." The woman pleaded that Sir Ramsay had "been through too much. He and the Missus!" "He loves her," she had said and, "He loved the other one too." She had screamed the poor girl's name when she went crashing down the stairs: "Angela!" And when it was over, she had cried, "Our beauty is dead! Just like Gabriella! What will Sir Ramsay say? It will break him!" Sherlock remembers wondering why the woman had not said that this death would break Lady Stonefield too. *If the Governor was somehow supporting this poor, unfortunate girl, then why did he not tell his wife? And if he did, why would she, who seems so close to her husband, not be hurt by the girl's death too? Was this girl a hidden love child from an extramarital affair? Did he keep that secret from her? But Lady Stonefield was so sad when I saw her, so united with him in grief.*

It is Sunday. The upper classes have established routines on the Sabbath. Usually, the Stonefields would attend church and then either visit friends or receive them in their home. But Sherlock is certain that word of the death of this invalid, somehow deeply connected to the Governor and whom he regularly visits, would have been sent to him almost immediately. He will know by this morning. Holmes doubts the Stonefields will be going anywhere after services today. Sir Ramsay will have locked himself in his study, hiding his distress from his wife.

The boy takes a moment to repeat his account of the occurrences in Hounslow to the apothecary, almost as if he can't believe them. The old man listens patiently. A big tear wells up in each of his eyes. "Dear, dear," he says to himself. When Sherlock finishes, they are both quiet for a moment. Then Holmes tells him what he intends to do now.

"You plan to go directly to Mayfair and speak to the Governor?"

"Yes, sir."

"But, why would he see you, and even if he did, why would he speak to you? And if he speaks to you, why would he want to dwell on what is obviously a tragic occurrence for him?

"He will."

The apothecary thinks for a few seconds. "Ah," he finally says, and the wisp of a smile slightly turns up the ends of his mouth.

But when Sherlock goes out the door, Sigerson Trismegistus Bell is disturbed. The boy is hiding something from him. He can feel it.

Holmes arrives in Mayfair in the early afternoon, well after church is over. He doesn't hesitate as he crosses the park in Hanover Square and moves across the street and right up to the big purple house and its fancy front door with the crescent window above it. He knocks.

It takes a while for someone to come, and when that gentleman does, he looks through the peephole for a very long while before he opens the door slightly. It is the butler, though only one eye is visible.

"Go away, boy!" he commands through the crack.

"I want to speak with Sir Ramsay Stonefield."

"Speak with him? You? Not in your lifetime!"

"If you do not announce me, you will do your master a grave disservice. Just show him my card."

Sherlock has taken one of his master's small cards –

SIGERSON TRISMEGISTUS BELL
APOTHECARY AND ALCHEMIST
DENMARK STREET, LONDON

and thoroughly scratched out the old man's name and written another, a single Christian name, on the other side. He shoves it through the crack toward the butler.

"I happen to know that Sir Ramsay is feeling under the weather today," says the boy.

"How could you –"

"He is in his study with the door closed. I am guessing you haven't seen him all day. I know *exactly* how he is feeling, and *why*."

The butler hesitates for a moment. Finally, he reaches through the door and takes the card between a thumb and forefinger, barely grasping it in his gloved hand, as if it were a piece of horse dung retrieved from the street. He quickly transfers it to a silver plate. "I shall show it to Sir Ramsay with my extreme apologies, and once he has shunned you, I shall return with two footmen and the groom and pitch you, with great violence, into the street." He waits for the poorly dressed boy's response, but the lad merely stands waiting. The door closes with a slam.

The butler is gone for less than a minute. He returns with a good deal of speed and opens the door abruptly. His face shows no emotion. "Follow me, sir!" he exclaims and leads Sherlock down the black-and-white tiled hallway to the stairs, then up its curving elegance to Sir Ramsay's study. Thrusting the door open, the butler exclaims, "The unnamed gentleman who handed me that card, sir!"

"Thank you, Brett. You may close the door."

"Yes, sir."

There is silence as the Governor, seated behind his huge mahogany desk, examines Sherlock. The man's eyes look red, his big gray sideburns and mustachios disheveled. His cravat is sloppily tied, as if he had undone it and then done it up again by himself. He is holding Holmes's card in his hand.

"How," he says in a very low voice, looking down at it, "do you know the name Angela?"

"I –"

"Are you the one who blackmailed me?"

They have never met.

"No, sir, but I know him well."

"Know him!" he pounds his fist on the desk.

"And I know all about your situation, everything," he lies. "I was there, in Hounslow last night, when she died."

"You were there!" Sir Ramsay's face grows red with anger and he glares up at Sherlock.

"But I have played no direct part in this."

The Governor's face softens. "My poor, abandoned daughter," he says and looks as if he is about to cry.

Daughter!

"I know about the other one too," says the boy, lying again.

"Our Gabriella!"

Our?

"Yes, sir."

The Governor gets to his feet and turns his back. He stares out the tall, latticed window over Hanover Square and Mayfair.

"Born with the faces of monsters! One cannot have that you know, not in our society. Lady Stonefield cannot be the mother of monsters. It will NOT do!" He turns and looks at Sherlock again. "Our society be damned, I say! But, I could not do it to her; I could not have her ridiculed. Lady Stonefield is a wonderful soul, you know. We have been through much with this."

There is a sudden knock on the door, though no one enters.

"Ramsay?" It is his wife on the other side.

"Yes, dear?" he calls out, glaring at Sherlock and putting his finger to his lips.

"Is everything all right? I heard shouting?"

"Not to worry, my dear. I am merely having a short conversation with a colleague, a little heated when it comes to a few fiscal issues but nothing to concern yourself about."

"On the Sabbath, Ramsay?"

Stonefield looks unsure of what to say, but finds the words. "That is the cause of the shouting, my dear. I am telling this chap that we will attend to this tomorrow. I was about to have Brett escort him out. I shall see you in the drawing room in a few moments. Is that all right, my love?"

"Yes, of course."

Her footsteps fade as she walks away.

"You haven't told her?" asks Sherlock "Why not?"

The Governor advances on him abruptly. "I thought you said you knew everything about my situation, sir. It does not sound like it. You would not have said that, had you known. I do not know who you are or what your purpose is, but Brett shall see you out this instant. If I ever even catch a glimpse of you –"

Say something or all is lost.

"It is in your interest to hear what I have to say, sir."

The Governor pauses.

"You have thirty seconds."

"You are correct. I do not know *all* about your situation. In fact, when I arrived, I knew just enough to get me through your door. I have learned a great deal more during the last minute or two."

"You have?"

"But here is what I do know, and it is of the greatest importance to you. I indeed know who is blackmailing you. He is a young man named Malefactor, though that is not his real name. I saw his true surname on an estate agent's contract just a year or more ago. It was difficult to read, scrawled as it was in his hand. But I committed that scrawl to memory and wrote it down afterward. I now believe his real name is Moriarty."

"Moriarty?"

"Yes. He controlled a street gang of adolescents in his youth for many years, using a dozen operatives, two of whom, Grimsby and Crew, were his ruthless lieutenants.

The former is the man he has blackmailed you into placing in Her Majesty's Treasury, and also the one who killed your daughter Angela. I was not lying when I said I was there last night."

"But who, sir, are you? And what do you want?"

"I am a half-Jew." The Governor stiffens. "I was treated as a leper by my peers from birth, despite my mother's high breeding and my father's genius. It was unfair, unjust. My mother was killed by a scoundrel, after I discovered that he had murdered a woman in Whitechapel. He killed my mother to stop me from revealing his identity. But I brought him to justice! Ever since that day I have vowed to bring villains like him to heel. Moriarty and his Grimsby and Crew are the worst of that sort. He is a genius, an angry and evil one with an ax to grind with life that he will work at forever if he is allowed. He intends to have his day in London, as the power behind the criminal menace."

"Where does he live? I shall have Scotland Yard collar him! There are people there who will keep quiet anything he has to say about me and put him away for good so that no one else will listen. Out with it, boy! Where can we find him?"

"I don't know. He is elusive in many ways."

"You don't know!"

"But I have some information and will do what I can to find out, and failing that I, uh, I shall move heaven and earth to stop him from maintaining Grimsby in a position of power. If I don't, both he and others will continue to infiltrate our government for many decades to come."

The Governor drops with a thump into his chair. "I must leave this Grimsby in his position. It does not matter that Angela is dead now. The shadowy Moriarty still knows our secret. His notes to me were very polite, very well written, ingenious really, but with dark and thorough intent. I am sure he secured proof of our predicament. Were I to dismiss Grimsby, he would reveal my secret to the world. I cannot do that to my wife." He seems about to weep.

"Tell me everything, sir, and I will do what I can."

Stonefield sighs. "There is not much else I can tell you. My wife gave birth to Gabriella first. The baby was horribly deformed. We were not sure what to do. We could not show our child to others in our society. As you know, such children are always given away. But we loved our poor creature. She was the result of our love. So, we pretended our child had died at birth, swore our doctor to silence, and kept her, attended to by the lady you met in Hounslow, and only her. Then we had our second child, Angela, and you cannot imagine my wife's distress when God or the Devil gave her to us even more deformed than her sister. We had considered operations for Gabriella and were hoping we might finally bring her out into the light of day for all to see, and be damned with them! But then, the second came. A second *monster* child! My wife could not be known as the mother of such a cursed breed."

"But, sir, they are your children."

"You are not in my position, young man, nor are you subject to the world my wife must inhabit."

Sherlock nods.

"There is one thing I cannot understand, sir. Why did the Hounslow woman say that this death would break only your heart, not your wife's, and why did you send Lady Stonefield away just now, and lie to her?"

"She does not know."

"That Angela is dead?"

"That they both are dead." He wipes a tear from his eye. "We *had* to do something with the children after Angela was born. We decided to give them away. I told my wife that I had sent them to a good family in Scotland who would care for them. Though it broke our hearts, we agreed to make it part of our past, never refer to it again, and be comforted by the fact that they were cared for and loved. But I could not completely send them away. I made up a reason to dismiss the woman you met in Hounslow and then paid her to tend to our children in her home. She and her husband are the kindest, most decent people on earth. I visit as often as I can. But Gabriella died of consumption a few years ago. You know the rest."

"Yes."

"You must go. I told my wife I was sending you on your way. I shall call Brett and he will discreetly escort you out. I will let him know to always take messages from you in the future. Thank you, young man. And I am sorry for the loss of your mother."

The Governor rings a bell and Brett appears. As the boy is about to leave, Stonefield stops him.

"One more thing. What is your name?"

"I am someone who is at your service, sir, and at the service of anyone who is wronged, whether they be rich or poor, Jew or Gentile, Englishman or otherwise." The boy straightens his second-hand frock coat. "My name is Sherlock Holmes."

13

INTO THE WEB

A plan is growing in Sherlock's mind, a secret plan. As he lies in his bed in the wardrobe that night, the horse-and-carriage sounds of London muffled outside the apothecary shop door, he thinks it through. His plan is a big one. It involves the complete destruction of Malefactor, his lieutenants, and all his future schemes, his entire career. The time has finally come for their confrontation.

The plan has already been set in motion. In order to accomplish the rest of it, the bulk of it, the most dangerous and difficult parts, he must play his role well. No one can know exactly what he is up to, not even Sigerson Bell. There is too much at stake. He shall tell him only what he needs to know.

But the next morning, a Monday, the old apothecary continues to sense that his charge is hiding something from him. They sit in the lab feasting on pigeon pie, goat cheese, and tea. Sherlock seems, to Bell, to be a little too forthcoming while explaining his next move. The boy is usually more cagey about his maneuvers, and the old man often has to draw them out of him. But today Holmes tells him everything, loudly and clearly.

"I shall drop by Her Majesty's Treasury this morning and confront Grimsby. I will have time to do that before I go to Snowfields. I have a class today."

"Do you think confronting him is wise? A public display?"

"I will loudly accuse him of the murder of Angela Stonefield."

The old man is mystified. It is unlike his brilliant boy to make such an error.

"But you must not. The Governor cannot have his secret revealed. Your enemy, this Malefactor chap, still has a hold on him, despite the girl's death."

"I shall not use her last name."

"I would not use any name, if I were you."

"Perhaps you are correct. And yet, I must go there. I must publicly remind him that I know something about him that has the potential to destroy him and his position, and that I intend to find a way to use it to do that very thing."

"Be careful what you say."

"Thank you, sir. I shall. I just wanted you to know that I was going there today to see him."

Bell lifts his red fez and scratches his balding pate after the boy goes out the door. Sherlock seems anxious and jumpy, also unlike him. But before the old man can give this much more thought, he begins to cough. This wretched spell lasts for ten minutes, the worst he has ever experienced. Afterward, he lies on the floor, barely able to move, and his handkerchief, gripped in his weak left hand, is full of blood.

Sherlock gets to Her Majesty's Treasury just as Mycroft arrives. The older brother looks at him with that same expression of concern that he's worn each time they've met here.

"Sherlock. Another pleasure. I have nothing to report about your old friend Mr. Grimsby. Surely you did not expect me to just swing into action concerning this. I must be very discreet, you know. And, as you also know, the last two days were not even working days. And yet, here you are. Have you made progress?"

"Oh, yes."

Mycroft notices a strange gleam in his younger brother's eyes.

"You say that with great confidence. Anything you might share?"

"No."

"How kind of you." He pauses. "Well, I must be on my way." He turns to go, but Sherlock takes him by the arm.

"I shall wait here to speak to Mr. Grimsby."

Mycroft wonders why his brother is telling him something that is painfully obvious.

"Yes, well, that is not a great shock, you know. But might I ask you to be gentle with him? Do not make a scene, I beg you."

"As you wish. I just wanted you to know that I intend to speak with him today."

"So you said."

Mycroft goes up the stairs into Her Majesty's Treasury, wondering about his brother's strange conduct.

Sherlock waits until almost every last employee of the Chancellor's office has arrived that morning. There is no sign of Grimsby. Reminding himself to return at closing time, he hurries off to Snowfields School, a long trip east all the way to the Old City and over London Bridge to Southwark.

When he returns, he again waits for the appearance of almost every Treasury employee and does not see the little henchman. Mycroft, one of the last to leave, spots him standing at the bottom of the stairs, leaning on a lamppost. The older brother reluctantly approaches, looking around.

"Your friend was not at his desk today."

"Really?"

"Curious, that. He has not missed a day yet."

"Curious, indeed. His superior was there, though, wasn't he? In good health?"

"Yes, he was," says Mycroft, giving his brother a quizzical look. "Shall you return tomorrow?"

"First thing."

"There is really no need, Sherlock. I can send a note around to you. Denmark Street, is it not? The old apothecary shop?"

"I shall be here."

"Well, if you must."

"I must."

And indeed he is. But this time, the instant Mycroft sees him, he approaches without hesitation.

"I've had distressing news. Someone told me coming up the street."

"What news?"

"This Grimsby, the chap you are seeking, he is dead."

Sherlock looks shocked. But there is a touch of acting in his reaction, almost as if he knew what Mycroft was going to say. Their mother was a singer and versed in the ways of the theater, and acting is a skill that Sherlock seems to have inherited from her.

"Really?"

"Yes, really, I'm sorry to say. He was missing and they found him in the Thames sometime early yesterday. It appears to have been foul play."

Sherlock can't resist a slight smile.

"Well, that doesn't become you. The young man is dead."

"And good riddance to him." Sherlock bows slightly to his brother. "It was lovely to see you again. Let us not be so long parted next time."

The boy almost skips off to school. He knows he shouldn't. It isn't right to celebrate a human being's death, any human being, even those hanged outside the Newgate Prison for detestable crimes, even little Grimsby. But that evening, when he tells Sigerson Bell, he again allows a slight smile to creep across his lips.

Bell, of course, notices it (because he notices everything) and is more than a little taken aback. He finds it difficult to make conversation on the subject after that and goes to bed wondering about his assistant.

Sherlock sleeps soundly that night, and when a knock comes at the door, before their breakfast and before the shop is even open, it is the old apothecary who answers. When he does, he lets out a yelp, a little like a war cry. But the person at the door shushes him, and the two of them make their way into the lab without a word. Holmes is just rising. When his bleary eyes see who is in the laboratory, his mouth opens wide and he can't close it.

"Hello, Sherlock."

Irene Doyle is standing beside Sigerson Bell. Or at least it looks like her. She is dressed, to the boy's mind, like an American. First of all, much to his consternation, the dress is cut low at the front, showing her lovely collarbones. A bustle sticks out prominently at her behind. There is frill and lace everywhere, the whole outfit made of silk, deep blue and red, bordered in white. She wears a matching bonnet and carries a parasol in one of her gloved hands. Her blonde hair is done up underneath her hat, and her face glows from little touches of color. She must be wearing some sort of high heel, since she seems taller than when he last saw her. Though his heart is now pounding, she looks relaxed. She is nearly seventeen years old, a young woman in her prime. She smiles at him.

"I – Irene."

Sigerson Bell slinks away with a smile, though he doesn't get very far. He stands just out of sight at the door to the main room. He is listening, of course.

"You are looking well," intones Sherlock, rather shakily.

"You've grown," she says, looking up at him.

"Thank you."

"I can't stay."

"Neither can I."

"Pardon me? You still live here, don't you?"

"Uh, I have things to do."

"Then we are in agreement."

"I suppose we are."

They are both silent for a moment.

"I thought I should stop by," says Irene, "and let you know how things have been with me. May I sit down?"

Sherlock gets her a stool. "Your letters have not been as frequent of late." In truth, he hasn't heard from her in months.

"I have been awfully busy." She begins tugging off her gloves, her long, elegant fingers sliding out one by one. "Did you . . . miss them?"

"Perhaps. A little."

"Then I shall write more often in the future."

"That means you are going back to America."

"For the time being."

"Time being?"

"I will live on the continent soon. There are opportunities in Europe."

"I see."

"But I will be in New Jersey for a few months first."

Sherlock can actually detect a slight accent in her speech.

"And, as usual, I will spend most of my days in New York City."

"I hear it is a fine town."

"It is the coming city in the world."

"Time will tell."

Irene's early letters had told of her settling in with a wealthy Newark family named Adler, the father a kind and serious-minded man. Mr. Doyle had met him on a business trip to London, learned of his connections in the singing world in New York City, and asked if he could help his ambitious daughter. Mr. Adler had responded with an offer to take her into his family home for a year and place her with some of the best singing teachers in America. It hadn't mattered to Mr. Doyle, or most certainly to Irene, that he was Jewish.

"My tutors have been wonderful. They have moved me forward. I have sung in some gorgeous halls lately."

"Well, that is what you want, it seems, so I am pleased for you."

"I have been just an opening act, of course. But more will come later. To Father's delight, I am far away overseas while I pursue my corrupt ways!" She laughs.

"So, you are set on your path?"

"Absolutely."

"And that path won't be in London?"

"Probably not, though I may be back from time to time. Why would you care anyway, Sherlock? Set on your own path, are you not? *All* alone?"

What if I told her that I need her?

He says nothing.

"I thought so."

"I –"

"I have made some remarkable friends, both women . . . and men."

The last word hits its mark and Sherlock says nothing again.

"I believe, more than ever, that it isn't right for women to be second-class citizens and be told what to do. I am going to make my own choices and friends, control my own life. I know that sounds selfish, but it shouldn't. Why can't women have the choices men have?"

"Men and women are different."

"Not inside."

Sherlock has been standing over her all this time. He pulls out the other laboratory stool and sits beside her. They are silent for a moment again. Finally, she takes him by the hand and squeezes it.

"So, what is your news?"

"I have little to report, I'm afraid. I am living the same pedestrian life."

"Staying out of trouble?"

"I am attempting to put off my career until I am truly ready. You know I tried to do that before. In fact, the last time I was in 'trouble,' as you put it, was when you convinced me to help with the Hemsworth dragon case."

"It didn't take much convincing."

"Oh, but you were good at it."

"We women can be. You should give in to us from time to time." She slaps him gently on the arm.

"I have my own way."

"And it is as hard and rigid as an iron walking stick."

"I believe there is nobility to my path. It is what must be done. It is what I must do. Justice is everything to me."

"But, right now, you are simply doing apothecary work?"

He hesitates.

"Oh, I see." She smiles. "Something is brewing! You were never able to lie to me. Have I come at a moment of excitement in your life? What is happening, Sherlock? Tell me."

He hesitates again. He cannot bring himself to tell her what has transpired this past week, and will definitely not reveal his plan. But there is one thing he can say, and he is pleased to do it.

"Grimsby is dead. It was likely foul play. Someone such as him dies no other way."

"Little Grimsby?" Her face flushes.

"Good riddance."

"Sherlock, no one's death should please you."

"This one does."

"But he was a helpless little one. All he knew was crime. He never had a chance, not the chances we had."

"Correction: *you* had. I had nothing and I chose a different path from that little bully. He was going to do much evil in his life. It is much better that he was snuffed out. His death has saved at least one life, maybe more."

"Sherlock, I know you thought me naïve when we first met and for a long time after. I know I miscalculated, somewhat, about Malefactor, but –"

"Yes, you did."

She closes her eyes in frustration with him; he need not have said that out loud. "But not entirely. I still believe, as father does, that all people can be reformed."

"And I do not."

"If you want to be a true seeker of justice, truly a good man, here's what I think you should do: search for Grimsby's murderer."

She doesn't get far with that idea. Sherlock won't discuss it. Soon he turns the conversation and there is no more talk of their careers, just a happier discussion about their pasts, their old friendship. They actually begin to laugh together. When it is time for her to leave, they are both reluctant to part. She kisses him on the cheek.

"I will be here for a week or more. Father spends much of his time with his *son*, so I am free most nights." The attention her father pays to her foster brother, Paul, the spitting image of his dead son, still grates on her. Her attachment to home has waned since Paul arrived. She smiles at Sherlock. "You know where to find me."

As she goes out the door, Holmes has the feeling that he wants to follow her, chase after her. But he stays inside. He sits down at the lab table.

"People keep stealing in and out of here, surprising

me!" he mutters to himself. *In the future, I need an upstairs flat of my own, with a companion and a housekeeper.*

"You know," says Sigerson Bell as he materializes out of the shadows like a ghost, not even pretending that he wasn't eavesdropping, "she is right. If you truly believe in justice, you should seek out the person who killed Grimsby. It would indeed mark you as what you say you intend to be."

An hour later, the boy is out on the streets. He has no school today. He wants to be alone for a while. He knows that his master and Irene are correct. If he were truly a good person, truly a man of justice, he would help to find Grimsby's murderer. But it is complicated, very complicated. He needs to sit somewhere and think about it. Usually, he takes his meals with Bell, but now he wants to find a public house for a long sit and then have some food on his own.

He heads to Leicester Square, walks past The Faustian Bargain where he once met with the famous young trapeze star, The Swallow, while in pursuit of the Brixton Gang, and finds another public house – a much calmer place called The Boy and Man.

He finds a booth, sits for a while, then orders a mug of tea and a chicken pot pie and starts to eat, losing himself in the meal and not thinking about what Irene and Bell had said. He thinks of Grimsby. *Dead.* But he can't help it; it doesn't sadden him in the least. There is, however, a small lingering feeling of guilt. *What if I indeed searched for his –*

"Master Sherlock Holmes, I perceive."

As if by magic, someone is sitting in the booth with him. Sherlock's head shoots up. Sunken eyes are looking back at him.

Malefactor! He has done it again.

"Wh-where did you come from?"

"Never you mind, Holmes. I can always find you." He sets his top hat on the table and takes off his gloves. He looks calm on the surface, but plucks at the gloves aggressively. Holmes can tell that he is holding back a seething anger.

"I can see that," says Sherlock.

"I prefer to be a mystery to you. You know too much about me already. In fact, in the future, should you live into the future, I think it would be best if you and I feign to have never known each other. It is best to have no past, no known past, at least."

"Agreed."

"But, as I say, you may not last much longer anyway. I don't know on how many occasions I have told you that I am not pleased with you."

"Once or twice."

"As we get older, I can assure you, the chances that you will survive my displeasure diminish substantially."

"You said almost as much before. This is about Grimsby."

"Not entirely. It is mostly about you."

"How so?"

"You, age sixteen and a half, have chosen, once more, to interfere in my affairs. I would have thought that you would have matured enough to know to stay out. As I have said to you before, we are not children anymore."

"At least one of us isn't."

"You state my case exactly. I did not know, the last time we met (and kick myself for not understanding), why you asked if I had been at my country home the night before. You were wondering if I, or one of my operatives, was following you in Hounslow, weren't you? I know that you discovered it was I who was blackmailing Sir Ramsay Stonefield and where the source of my inside knowledge lived."

"I did indeed."

"That is most unfortunate. Though Grimsby, that little turncoat, has hurt our immediate chances with the police and in government by his treachery, they are not at an end. I shall get my way. I shall be an influence at every level of London life."

Malefactor's face had turned red when he mentioned Grimsby. That intrigues Sherlock, greatly.

"I have no doubt that you think you can do as you please in that regard," says Holmes. "But concerning Grimsby, you seem angry. No grieving on your part?"

Malefactor springs to his feet. "That little pig! He was not loyal! He has made great troubles for us!"

Sherlock is even more intrigued.

Holmes's enemy doesn't wait for him to respond. He turns on him. "Never mind about Grimsby! He got his due! Live by the sword and you will die by it. Stay away from all of this, Sherlock Holmes! I am warning you for the *last* time! Stay away!"

As Malefactor stalks out of the public house, Holmes is radiant. He has a new plank in his plan, a brilliant one. He will indeed search for Grimsby's murderer. And when the police consider the facts that he will unearth, it will be obvious to them that the murderer was either Malefactor or his only living lieutenant, Crew; or both. *I can do more than just put them behind bars.* He almost vibrates with excitement. The opportunity is suddenly before him to provide evidence that will see his archenemy *hanged*!

14

AFTER CREW

Sherlock has to go back to school the next day. He will begin his investigation of Grimsby's murder the instant he is finished. He tells the apothecary what he is up to.

"Why, my young knight, are you constantly telling me what you are about to do? That is not like you."

Holmes is usually so secretive that the old man has to draw things out of him.

"Really? Not like me? You think so?"

"I know so."

Sherlock ignores the comment. He is a man on a mission. "I will begin at Scotland Yard."

"Young Lestrade?"

"Absolutely. I am guessing that he has seen the body."

When Sherlock Holmes arrives at police headquarters in Whitehall Street at about five o'clock in the afternoon, he is sure that he will find Lestrade there, even though many of the other constables and detectives on his time shift will have left for the day. The young sleuth is just that dedicated, especially since he became the only Lestrade on the Force. He needs to build his career. This is a godsend to Holmes.

Though Sherlock hasn't been actively attempting to solve crimes since he played his part in the Hemsworth-Nottingham magicians' affair, he has been, as has been his custom for a year or so, helping young Lestrade, both by bringing him cases and ideas and listening to him when he has a problem. It is an excellent strategy – he is making sure that the aspiring detective will always be an ally at Scotland Yard. And for now, their partnership gets him access through the front door whenever he wants. The desk sergeant no longer attempts to toss him into the street.

The minute Sherlock asks to see Lestrade Junior, he is allowed into his office. It is far down the building, at the back, past all the desks and clutter, distant from where his father used to reign in a big room at the front, with its huge map of London on the wall. The son's kingdom isn't much larger than a broom closet.

He is twenty years old now, though still not fully capable of growing the kinds of whiskers he is attempting to proliferate on his slightly ferret-like face – an unfortunate visage, not entirely dissimilar to his father's. He may have to give up his hirsute ambitions or settle for a modest mustache. He is wearing a tweed suit again, the one he wears every day, almost as if this imitation of his father's similar bad taste will somehow help him in his pursuit of criminals. He is at his desk and actually smiles when Holmes enters.

This, despite the fact that the younger boy now towers over him, a fact that he tries not to dwell upon.

"What have you today?" he asks.

"It is what *you* have that interests me."

Young Lestrade doesn't like Sherlock's tone. And there is an expression in his eye today that was often there when he was in active pursuit of his own solutions to cases. The last time Lestrade saw this look was during that magicians' investigation. But there is something else about the lad that is worrisome.

"I have an interest in the Grimsby case."

Lestrade is momentarily relieved, pleased to hear that this is just about Grimsby. The young detective knows that Sherlock has some sort of relationship, or enmity, with the former street gang leader named Malefactor (though that rough has apparently reformed now and hasn't been seen in years) and would have known Grimsby well. "Yes, of course, I should have thought of that."

"I would like to see the body."

"Uh . . ."

"I will tell you all that I know of this case in return." Sherlock will, of course, do no such thing. He will reveal to Lestrade *only* what he wants him to know.

"You are aware, Holmes, that I would do anything for you in a professional way, just *about* anything that is, but this is really against police protocol."

"And?"

"And that means it can't be done."

"Lestrade, you cherish your rise in the ranks of this police force, do you not?"

The detective, again, does not like the look in Sherlock Holmes's eyes.

Ten minutes later they are downstairs in the dank-smelling basement of Scotland Yard, which the Force keeps as a temporary morgue before bodies are sent off for burial in London's many graveyards. Sherlock wants to see the corpse today since he knows it will be in the ground as soon as tomorrow. Visiting cemeteries, for *any* reason, is not one of his favorite things – it has been even less so since his parents died. Unearthing a body (as the city's creepy body-snatchers often do and Sigerson Bell has paid for on occasion) would not be something he would *ever* want to be part of. Though some of London's richer graveyards are respectable and pleasant to tour, most are festering fields of decaying flesh and disease. In fact, the location of many has been forgotten by authorities, and skulls are always turning up, sometimes as the equipment for stick and ball games that children play. Grimsby will likely be dumped in some such godforsaken place. Sherlock tries not to think of it.

When the rough old sackcloth is pulled off the little criminal, Holmes is almost immediately overpowered with guilt. In death, with all the care gone from Grimsby's face and the evil intentions not present in his eyes, his appearance is that of a young man in an adolescent's body. A mere child, destined to be nothing, brutally murdered. Sherlock can't believe how small he looks.

"This was not suicide," says Lestrade. "He was killed, no doubt in a desperate fight or brawl of some sort. We know little else. There are actually no visible signs of injury to him at first glance. You only see them when you pull up his shirt."

Lestrade does so and reveals a nasty purple ring across Grimsby's chest. Sherlock actually turns away. That isn't like him. It surprises Lestrade.

"Getting squeamish in our old age, are we?"

"Not at all." Sherlock turns back.

"As I say, we are not exactly sure how this was done. But he had no money on his person, no purse. So, we assume that it was robbery."

"Or meant to look like it."

"We are considering that too, of course."

"You won't do much about this, will you?"

"Well, no, you know how it goes, Sherlock. We don't have the resources, and this is a poor boy whose death is not particularly important."

"Where was he found?"

"A mudlark pulled him from the river near St. Katherine's Docks, Wapping."

Sherlock knows what mudlarks are – he has seen them plying their trade many times down by the Thames, picking up things that others throw out on the shoreline or dragging the river from their boats attempting to find their kind of gold: dead bodies at the ends of their hooks, pockets filled, they hope, with something that can be sold, or simply corpses of some value to the Force.

"Anything else?" asks Lestrade, who is obviously anxious to leave.

Sherlock looks closely at the body again.

"Where was the corpse taken when it was found?"

"To St. Bartholomew's Hospital, simply for a quick analysis. If that is everything, we really should be going."

"That is sufficient, for now."

Back in Lestrade's office, they say good-bye. Sherlock doesn't linger. He is soon out the door and down the hallway toward the foyer. But he stops part way and returns. Lestrade looks up.

"Something else?"

"Do you record a meeting like ours?"

"Pardon me?"

"Do you note in your records that I came to see the body and that I will be investigating this in order to solve the crime, find the murderer?"

"What a strange question."

"Do you?"

"Well, normally I might. But this is not a normal situation. I am not allowed to have ordinary citizens into the morgue to look at corpses. You well know that."

"But you could say that I knew the deceased and thus my observation of the body was helpful to you in your pursuit of the culprit."

"Even though we aren't *really* pursuing him?"

"Yes."

"But that is absurd."

"Were you to get into any trouble over this – I observed

that a few people saw us slip through the door that leads down to the morgue – you would then have an excuse."

"I suppose you are right."

"You should also note that, as I mentioned, I too am anxious to have the murderer found."

"I don't see how that is pertinent, but I shall do as you say, as a queer favor." Lestrade waves him off. "Now go away, Sherlock. You are acting strange today. I'm guessing this has something to do with your strategy on this case?"

Sherlock smiles. "Absolutely."

"Well then, pursue it, without my official approval, but keep me informed."

"Oh, I shall."

Holmes walks out onto Whitehall Street, enthralled. He has learned a great deal. He notices Her Majesty's Treasury a few buildings down and across the road. It looks quiet. Many of its employees have left for the day. He crosses over and sits on its steps, thinking.

I want Malefactor and Crew hanged. But he recalls what Lestrade said about Grimsby's murder, the official police line. "We assume that it was a robbery." *I have to prove them wrong. They must believe it to be an assassination: a brutal killing performed by a vicious thug at Malefactor's angry request. That thug could very well have been Crew.*

"Sherlock?"

Mycroft Holmes is coming down the steps, one of the last Treasury employees on his way home. Though, as usual, he slows when he sees his brother, this time he actually doesn't seem entirely displeased.

"I can say with sincerity that I am glad to see you today. I have done some legwork for you, my boy."

"Legwork?"

"This Grimsby fellow. I had someone in the hiring department look into his situation. This detecting thing is great fun when you give it a try!"

"His situation?"

"It seems Ronald Loveland lived in a recently let home on Doughty Street."

That's to the north, thinks Sherlock, *just north of Bloomsbury, not far from where Irene lives on Montague Street.* The address doesn't surprise him. Malefactor's brain and Holmes's work similarly, or at least they come to the same conclusions when at the game of crime or fighting it. It isn't a particularly rich neighborhood, but it is a nice, reasonable place for decent people with decent occupations. That makes perfect sense – Malefactor wouldn't have been spending too much money on Grimsby, but had the Treasury authorities come by that neck of the woods, they would have been sufficiently impressed. From there, Grimsby was close to the action in Whitehall, just a healthy walk away, but not too close for his movements to be observed by anyone from work on a regular basis. It is also not known as an area where government employees live. He would have had enough privacy to conduct his other life.

"Is this helpful to you?" asks Mycroft. But his younger brother seems distant.

Sherlock tries to imagine how he might build a case around this information. *Malefactor or Crew, or both, came to quiet Doughty Street, where only they and the Treasury hiring department knew Grimsby could be found, most likely in a barren house let for him, without a spot of furniture, pennies pinched. One of them murdered him there, leaving that welt on his chest, and then took him many miles to Wapping and threw him into the Thames. Does that make sense? Is it not believable that this murder, with its violent wound, was performed by someone who knew Grimsby and his location, a crime of revenge and passion? Or . . .*

"No."

"No?"

"I am sorry, Mycroft. Thank you for your efforts. But I must be going."

Sherlock almost leaps to his feet.

Enough with Grimsby's residence or even with him, period! Enough with theories! It doesn't matter where he lived! Malefactor or Crew or another of their thugs performed the ugly deed: That is the only conclusion worth considering. And of those roughs, it certainly makes sense that the physically powerful and pitiless Crew was the culprit. That is my starting point, no other.

"I shall see you again, Mycroft, uh, sometime soon."

Sherlock starts striding quickly away, up Whitehall toward Trafalgar Square. The older Holmes stands silent on the steps of the Treasury, interrupted in his detective career and thrown by his brother's erratic behavior.

Sherlock breathes hard as he walks, and his mind is teeming. *I must simply find Crew and see if I can prove that he, and no one else, did it, and that Malefactor was supporting him both financially and strategically! Do NOT make this complicated.*

The time has come to get further into his enemy's brain and find Crew's lair. Sherlock doubts that such a nest is in an even remotely respectable part of town. It will be far from Doughty Street.

I know where to look.

The first thing he knows he must do is disguise himself again, and in a different way. There is no question that Malefactor and his people will be following him, are likely even observing him now. He glances around Trafalgar Square as he marches through it and then moves briskly toward the apothecary shop. *It is time to act!*

When Sherlock tells his master what he intends to do that night, the old man looks worried. It takes him a moment before he responds.

"Well, if you go through with this, we must disguise you again. You cannot pursue Mr. Crew while being followed by you-know-who."

The boy smiles. He and Sigerson Bell are thinking in tandem again.

"I am guessing you should be a thug!" cries the old man.

"You are guessing correctly."

An hour later, an hour of great fun for the two friends, they have Sherlock dressed as though he were a member of the Trafalgar Square Irregulars. Choosing expertly from Bell's stock of clothing, they soon have him dressed in rags. He wears a tattered old navy pea jacket, an oily soft cap pulled down tightly over his face, and is long-haired, soot-stained, and even smelling of fish, since Sherlock believes his search must begin in the East End in Whitechapel and move from there down toward the river, the Tower of London, and the docks. That is where the greatest number of criminals make their grimy residences. It is also near where Grimsby's body was pulled from the Thames.

They wait until darkness comes. This doesn't please Bell – he knows that criminals come out at night. But he also knows that this is exactly when the boy must do his work, when his search will be most productive.

In order to get Sherlock out of the house undetected, they once again perform the little feat they employed to twice spring him from the shop this past week. Together, they become the hugely Fat Man one last time, with the emaciating Bell inside Sherlock's massive trousers, clutching his chest. Anyone casing the apothecary shop from the outside would assume that this big man is now a regular pedestrian on Denmark Street. But this time Holmes is upset when they are glued together. He can tell that his mentor has lost weight even in the last few days and, when they are moving, he can feel his bony chest heaving as he coughs inside the costume. Bell's days are numbered to a very few. The boy is so distraught that he wants to turn around. But he knows the old man would not like that. They go out the secret entrance in the back and hail a hansom cab on Crown

Street. They send it down to Trafalgar Square and east on Fleet Street, up the hill and past the magnificent Cathedral. When they stop near London Bridge, only the boy gets out, looking for all intents and purposes like a street thug. The cab turns around and heads back to Denmark Street, while Sherlock makes his way up to Whitechapel Road and into those warren-like streets and alleys to its south, where all of London knows that danger lurks.

15

UNDERGROUND

There are fewer gaslights in Whitechapel, and Sherlock can feel tension in the air. There aren't many pedestrians in the streets now either. All the working-class people have gone home to early beds so they can rise before dawn to pursue their brutally hard lives. Almost no one above their class ever comes to the East End, unless perhaps safe inside a carriage to attend the Garrick Theatre or some such place of entertainment. But even those folks never leave their carriages to walk the streets, either on their way into these neighborhoods or out.

Sherlock, of course, is on foot. His disguise, the calculated look of danger in his appearance and attitude, is part of what will protect him, and he is well aware of it.

He is searching for inhabitants who may know Grimsby or Crew.

This nightly adventure isn't something new to Sherlock. Though Sigerson Bell doesn't always know it, Holmes has taken to walking the streets of London at night alone over the past year or so, learning all of it – its rookeries, its wealthy areas, its nooks and crannies, all the strange people who move about in it after the sun goes down. It is part of his training, so he works at it with unwavering attention. He must be willing to risk his life when he gets older, so he might as well begin now. He has learned to spot criminal elements at a glance. Sometimes when he walks, he thinks of Dickens. He has heard it said that the novelist used to do exactly this – walk the streets for hours at night, sometimes taking in twenty miles or more at a time. It was as if, like Sherlock, he were on a mission, a need to reveal the truth about this glorious and inglorious city, this good and evil place.

Holmes makes his way south toward the river. Grimsby was thrown into the Thames, and the boy doubts that it would make sense to a court that someone could be murdered and then carried more than a few hundred yards to the water, let alone several miles. At least, it wouldn't be believable that an assassination would have happened that way. It had to have been planned. And good planning by Malefactor or Crew would entail disposing of their target as quickly as possible. It needed to be fast and clean.

In minutes he can smell the river. Though he is still a good distance off and in little streets with pungent sewage running down the narrow foot pavements, he can smell that fishy, metallic odor that rises from the mighty Thames.

The Tower of London, looking ominous, is south and to his right, and the sprawling London docks are just ahead to his left. He is entering the center of London's criminal world, an area where the police seldom venture, where they get in and get out, and only when they must.

The buildings along here are ancient – stone and brick

– all of them looking black or gray, built up close to the road, forming veritable walls that make the streets look like frightening tunnels. The rancid yellow fog is heavy. People come in and out of it, appearing suddenly right near the boy. At times he can barely see anything – sounds and smells predominate. He hears babies crying from the open windows, sees children with almost green-colored skin walking past in rags as if half asleep. Ladies of the night, appearing nothing like ladies and more like sea hags, smile toothless grins at him. But he knows not to look directly at anyone. He moves quickly, as Dickens did, noting everything but dwelling on nothing. He is well aware of what he is looking for.

Not long before he reaches the docks, he finds it. On a tight corner in a little gray courtyard outside a grimy coffee house or sandwich shop (it is hard to tell which it is, and hard to imagine anyone frequenting it since no food seems evident), a group of men huddle on the foot pavement. No one comes near them. No one dares. Every one of them looks like the illustrations of Bill Sikes, the bad man from *Oliver Twist* who murdered his sweet Nancy with his bare hands. They are dressed in layers of clothing despite the warm, misty night. They wear big boots and heavy coats, filthy rags around their throats, dirty hats, from felt caps to toppers. Sherlock nears. His heart begins to pound. *I must speak to them. I must summon the courage. That is the only way. It will be all right in the end. I must have my fists ready, my Bellitsu, act older. I can do it.*

"Bottom of the evening to you, blokes," he says, keeping his voice in the lower registers it sometimes occupies these days. He tips his hat and comes to a halt. His accent is working-class Irish.

The men had been murmuring. They grow silent.

"And whot if it is, you Mick?" says the biggest one.

"I is looking for a chap."

For now, the men appear impressed enough that he is speaking to them, so they don't make a move to hurt him. They seem to think they recognize a fellow blackguard.

"Well, we ain't in the business of finding 'im," says another one.

"Unless," says a third, "you can makes it worth our worthwhiles."

They all laugh.

"And if you can't," adds the big one, "then we mays 'ave to find you a place in St. Saviour's Cemetery."

Sherlock knows that they aren't interested in his clothing. When you walk through this area at night, you mustn't wear anything that anyone would want. You could be beaten and stripped bare. His clothes are so grimy and soot-stained that they aren't any better than what these men are wearing. But what they think he might have inside his attire is likely of interest. The boy needs to be ready for that.

"Spare any coins?" laughs one of them as they begin to try to surround him. Sherlock shifts so his back is to the building. Bell taught him to do that in the early days of his self-defense instructions. It is a cardinal rule.

"If you have more than one gentleman to deal with," the old man had sputtered, dressed in his bizarre fighting outfit (which included his hideous sparring tights), the sweat pouring off his bandanna-draped forehead like it was coming out a breaking dam, "always keep everyone of them in front of you. The same thing in an establishment of any sort – find a chair with its back to the wall."

The big one seems to notice Sherlock's subtle defensive maneuver. He is likely a street fighter of some skill. He doesn't say anything, but the boy can tell by his expression that he glimpsed the move and is impressed.

"I ain't carrying anything you lot would like, except me fists," says Holmes.

"Is that so?" grins a little one, advancing on him.

"'Old your 'orses," says the big one, "let's 'ear 'im gab. There ain't many who would talk to us on their lonesome. Let's give 'im a chance."

Sherlock stares right back at the little one, who seems to be emboldened by being in a group.

"I can defend meself, friends. I don't cares that much 'ow long I live, so much as I live an interesting life to me last breath. If one of you . . . for example, you, sir," he speaks right at the little one, never moving his gray eyes from him, "was to attack me, I would be satisfied with just cutting off your nose, I would, and perhaps with shoving it in your gob before you all accosted me. That would give me satisfaction and take me to me maker with a smile upon me face."

Sherlock puts his hand into his deep trousers pocket to grip his horsewhip, shoving part of it forward in the material to make it look like the business end of a knife. The light goes out in the little one's eyes. He even takes a step backward. The others stop coming forward too. The big one actually smiles.

"Who might you be looking for? We knows every bloke worth knowing."

"A fellow named Malefactor."

There is absolute silence. In fact, even in the dim gaslight in the fog, Sherlock can see a look of fear flicker across the big one's face. Then he swallows so hard that his Adam's apple is evident moving in his throat. Sherlock expects someone to say something soon. But no one utters a word. It shocks the boy. He knew that Malefactor's influence had been great on the streets in the old days and that it had grown of late, but he never dreamed that it would stop the very voices of East End criminals. *Already*, he thinks.

The silence continues. Finally, Sherlock speaks.

"What about a man named Crew?"

"You best be moving on," says the big one, in a voice that actually trembles.

Holmes doesn't need a written invitation. He backs away, keeping his face toward them until he is at the end of the street. When he turns, he moves as fast as he can go without running. But when he gets two blocks away, closer to the river, a face suddenly appears in front of his out of the fog. The man had rounded a corner and almost bumped into him.

It is the big thug. His chest is heaving as if he has been running.

"That ain't a question you asks on the streets. Who is you?"

"Anonymous," says Sherlock Holmes, and he employs

the big word without his low-Irish accent. In fact, he pronounces it carefully and clearly.

"I knows what that means," says the thug, "and I knows you ain't that. You IS someone. But if you 'ave a beef with that man you mentioned back there, that power, then you 'ad best give it up. His lieutenant, a devil not much bigger than a midget, went by the name of Grimsby, was murdered round 'ere just short days ago. It weren't done the way it should 'ave been done. There were something not right about it, a killing more vicious than even we would do. Word is that man you mentioned, 'e 'ad it done."

"Malefactor?"

The man won't respond.

"By the hand of Crew?" asks Sherlock. "Do the streets say it was Crew?"

"All I can say of a man by that name is that I 'ave seen 'im. Big 'un, extra fat on him, blonde 'air and blue eyes, narrow brush mustache, never says nothing, and very queer. But I don't really know nothing 'bout 'im, don't know where 'e lives or what 'e does, 'cept 'e is connected to that there other man you mentioned. And as for the murder, the streets is silent about things such as that. I could tell you were different back there, but whoever you is, copper or villain or worse, I would leave this be."

"Tell me more."

But the man vanishes into the fog. Sherlock pursues him in a mad rush, barely able to see. As he does, he thinks about what else the man might be able to tell him if he asked the right question. Heart pounding, chest heaving, catching up, losing the man, and spotting him ahead now and then as he runs away down the little streets and around corners, the right query comes to the boy.

Suddenly, the man completely disappears. And it isn't because he has turned another corner, entered an establishment, or taken to his heels with greater effectiveness. He simply was standing in a spot on the road and then vanished.

Sherlock rushes up to the place and sees a circular, heavy-iron grating about three feet in radius in the foot pavement right next to a building. One has to look closely to see it. The man obviously pulled it back, went down into it, and then returned it to its place from beneath. Holmes looks around and then does the same.

When he dangles his legs into the underground, his feet reach rungs. Down a ladder he goes and finds himself in a tall, circular passageway tiled with brick. The smell is horrible. Big pipes run along the floor. He knows that he is very close to the river now, in the sewers, the magnificent new conduits built by the queen's brilliant engineer Joseph Bazalgette. There are more than a thousand miles of them passing under London to move the city's excrement into the water far downstream, instead of having it dumped in the streets to run into the Thames near where the populace lives, giving them cholera and a host of other diseases. Sherlock remembers Bell muttering about this, saying that it should have been done centuries ago.

Though impressed by his surroundings, the boy has no time to admire the engineering. He hears voices ahead, and scuffling, as if more than one person were moving at a brisk pace up there. Sherlock begins to run. For a while, the big rats out ahead of him try to get away. They scurry through the sewers as if they know them, up and down its short iron staircases, around corners, avoiding pipes, crouched over through the tighter parts of the system. But eventually, they stop.

Sherlock halts too, and then carefully approaches.

It is the same men he had encountered on the street. They seem at home down here, as if this were a common place for them to meet. They have obviously decided that whoever is following them can be faced now, deep in the tunnels. There are seven of them against Sherlock Holmes. They don't seem to be worried about his knife anymore.

The big one steps forward.

"You is trying our patience. I told you clear – we cannot talk about the man you seek. No one can. You must leave or we will 'urt you. You must leave now!"

The others advance on Holmes. Two in particular seem to truly want at him.

But Sherlock has had enough of this. It is time to act. He pivots in perfect Bellitsu motion, executing an Oriental move that the apothecary has made him practice hundreds of times and that these thugs have never seen on London streets, marshals the power in his legs and hip by twisting, and drives the sole of his boot into the chest of the first man. Not a little fellow, he is nevertheless driven back by the blow as if he were shot from a cannon. He flies six feet backward and smacks into the wall, his spine hitting first and then the base of his skull. He is instantly semi-conscious and slides down the wall into a partially sitting position. Sherlock knows that the second man will go for his weapon to neutralize it first. ("Always imagine what your opponent is about to do!" Bell had often screamed at him in the midst of their battles.) The boy seizes the man by the arm that darts at his trousers' pocket. He pulls him close, and in an instant has that arm in a "bar," forcing it in two different directions, about to snap it in half. The man cries out in pain and asks for mercy.

"Stand back!" Sherlock shouts at the others, "or I will break it!"

The other men stop. The big one can't resist a grin.

"What else do you wants? Ask us for something simple, and we will tell you. There are things we can't speak of, because we fear that man you mentioned more than we will ever fear you. But if there is something we can tell you that will release my accomplice 'ere and satisfy you, then we will try."

Sherlock knows what to ask. It was what came to him while pursuing this fellow up on the streets. He had plucked it from his memory.

"There was a man, an operative in the Brixton Gang, arrested a few years ago in Rotherhithe, nominally for robbing the Crystal Palace and for the attempted murder of Monsieur Mercure. He squealed on his fellow gang members to the Force and before the magistrates. For that, for putting his brothers away for a very long time, causing even the execution of one of the gang's two leaders, the evil and most murderous of their lot, one Charon, whom the police were desperate to destroy, this man was allowed to go free after two years. He has been at liberty for some months now. I know of that gang and its members." Sherlock taps his finger to the side of his temple. "I know them by name and appearance. I was instrumental in bringing them to justice. I heard, through sources, of the freeing of one of their number, but I do not know who that was, *which* one, or *where* he is. He is plainly a man of few scruples, one who can be bought, and one whose exact whereabouts are protected by the police. But the streets know things. You may not have all the information I need, but I am guessing you know something. If you can tell me anything about this turncoat, it may lead me in the direction I need to go. You would be telling me nothing directly about Malefactor or Crew. The Brixton Gang was as well connected as any in the criminal world. It is my theory that this man, this squealer, knows something of Crew and his location. And he may be the only one of your like who would actually tell me. I must speak with him."

The big thug hesitates for a moment, calculating. Sherlock tightens his grip on the other man's arm, bringing another cry of agony from him.

"That slime was the other leader. He's a clever rat . . . name is Sutton."

"Ah, Sutton!" remarks Holmes, remembering that night in Rotherhithe. "Sutton himself!"

"I am told he lives to the east somewheres, though some says south, in a small town. No one 'as found the squeak yet, but we will!"

"Not before I do. But thank you, sir. You have been most helpful."

Within moments Sherlock Holmes has vanished from their sight and is hot-footing it home to the apothecary's shop.

Holmes has always feared Crew. His size, his silence, and the deadness in his eyes speaks of a soul that, unlike Grimsby, who appeared to have fallen into his circumstances from hard beginnings, is truly evil, born that way. Sherlock realizes how little he really knows about Crew. He doesn't even know his first name.

Where in the world would such a man live? And do I REALLY want to find him, somewhere in a lair in these streets, with HIS back to the wall?

16

SOMETHING INHUMAN

In the morning, Sherlock Holmes once again tells Sigerson Bell every single thing that he has just done concerning the case. He explains what happened on the streets the previous night and gives him a detailed analysis of what he intends to do next. The old man receives the information with a shake of his head.

"You neglected to tell me precisely when you urinated this morning and have yet to inform me of exactly how many breaths you took since the last hour struck."

But despite the humor in his reaction, underneath he is beginning to ponder in a deeper way why his young charge is operating in this manner. An idea has come into his head and it worries him. He barely thinks it possible.

Sherlock isn't at school today, so he has it all to himself to continue the search for Crew in earnest. His first stop is Scotland Yard. He needs answers to two questions. After that, he doubts he will require Lestrade anymore. He hopes he can do the rest himself.

"Ah, Sherlock!" says Lestrade, not nearly as happy as his tone.

"Just two questions," says the boy, barely looking at his ally as he rushes through the doorway. He begins to pace in the office's tight quarters, his head down, his eagle nose to the floor, nostrils flaring, gray eyes darting back and forth. He is like a restless hound sniffing for the fox, knowing the scent is near, the chase getting hotter. "You said that Grimsby's body was taken to St. Bartholomew's Hospital first, before it was brought here?"

"Yes."

"To which medical man?"

"Sherlock, I can't –"

The boy holds a finger up to his lips, as if trying to keep back his anger and impatience, hold back the oaths he'd like to shout, angry that this inconsequential detective is hesitating to tell him what he must know.

"Which doctor?!"

"The same as we always use."

Sherlock shouts at him. "Tell me, Lestrade! Now!"

Lestrade is shocked at the look on his face. The veins have come out on his neck and forehead. He knows this boy to be eccentric and driven. But now he seems almost possessed. Lestrade closes the door to his office, and gives up the name.

"Doctor Craft."

"Thank you. Now, you must tell me something else, something much more delicate, so delicate that you will want to say that you can never tell me. But you must." He is pacing even faster.

"What is it?" Lestrade dreads the answer.

"I want to know the whereabouts of one Sutton, formerly of the Brixton Gang."

Lestrade's mouth drops.

"Imagine," says Sherlock, before the young detective can say a word, "that life is a very narrow thing and that, when one thinks, one always thinks narrowly. It is like that for the majority of people. Thus, let us imagine that when most of us think, we function as though our thoughts were in a box or a carton of some sort and that we could not possibly ever allow them to be outside of that container. But, if we were to *really* want to be different, to get things done in a way that others don't allow, then we, we who are different and really want to achieve, must think outside of that container."

"I have no idea what you are talking about, Sherlock, but I can't –"

Holmes's face turns crimson. "Then know that if you do not do this for me I shall never speak to you again! And that you, sir, will occupy this tiny little office for the rest of your career, instead of the big one your father had, instead of becoming the premier inspector in the world's greatest police force!"

Lestrade can't believe the color of Sherlock's face. It is fear of that more than anything else that causes him to blurt out two facts.

"He goes by the name of Hopkins, in Rochester."

Rochester is to the east of London. *East,* just as the biggest street thug said. *They are closing in on him,* thinks Sherlock. *I must move fast.*

Holmes saves almost every penny that Bell gives him and has enough in his purse to take a train to Rochester and back. There will be many going in that direction today from London Bridge Station on the London, Chatham & Dover Railway line. Sherlock knows that for a certainty – this past year, he has begun memorizing the train schedules. St. Bartholomew's Hospital is to the east, in the City, the old part of London. He will go there on his way to the station.

The doctor saw the body immediately after it was found. The police have only vague theories. But Craft will know something about that nasty welt across the little villain's chest – the wound the killer left behind. Has he ever seen anything like it? What exactly, in his mind, killed Grimsby? Does he think it was some unusual weapon, or technique, some machine? Or was it something else? Most importantly, can I connect Crew to it?

The boy walks back along Fleet Street and swings north before he reaches St. Paul's and the London Wall. He smells the meaty odor of the Smithfield Market and slows. He is almost there. If he had a choice, he wouldn't go to St. Bartholomew's Hospital at all. He knows that being inside its walls will upset him. He stops for a moment on Charterhouse Street, listening to the shouts and the bellows of the animals in the market.

He remembers the first time he was in Bart's. It was three years ago, in the spring of 1867, when he sneaked in to see Irene after she was nearly killed by the Whitechapel murderer's coach. Sherlock had caused that nearly fatal accident, just as he had caused the death of his mother. To be more precise, his friendship with Irene had caused it. She had been targeted by his enemies. And so, to protect her, he had pushed her away – the beautiful and dynamic Irene, now resident in America, soon to be in Europe, *never* to be with him.

He steels himself and banishes all thoughts of Irene Doyle. He must go to Bart's, get inside, and find what he needs to find. What he is doing today must be his priority. He cannot live in the past. *I must never look backward.*

The hospital is so huge that it takes up several blocks, a monster building with tentacles everywhere, made of brick and rather ominous, looking in places as old as the many hundred years it is said to be. He finds the arched entrance through which he passed when he went to see Irene. He knows his way inside these two big wooden doors. Assuming that Dr. Craft will be somewhere upstairs, where Sherlock recalls that the chemical laboratories are, he passes the big outpatient room on the main floor, hears moans from patients, and flies up the big stone steps to the first floor. Here the halls are wide and whitewashed and everything smells of medicine. He remembers spotting several labs down one particular hall. He finds it and is relieved to see that he won't have to pass the Accident Ward where Irene convalesced. He keeps his head down and doesn't look into the eyes of the nurses who pass and only lifts his head when he nears the laboratories. The doors are tall and wooden, going almost all the way to the ceiling. A feeling of excitement begins to fill him, and not just because he feels he may be nearing the doctor who first examined Grimsby's body. Laboratories *always* arouse him. Bell has taught him everything he knows about chemistry, and the boy adores it. There is nothing better for both of them than experimenting with the chemicals and alkaloids in the old man's modest lab. He thinks of the space, equipment, and materials available in this, the largest of London's hospitals. It almost makes him shake with excitement. *Imagine being allowed in here to experiment!* He considers the things he could learn, the theories he could test, the gruesome crimes he could solve with such a place as his ally.

In his reverie, he actually begins to walk past the chemical laboratory door that bears Craft's name. But someone comes out of the entrance and walks right into him.

"Oh, I beg your pardon," says the man.

Sherlock looks at him. *Age seventeen or eighteen, a student, not ambitious, wants to be an assistant of some sort here, perhaps a dresser.* Holmes observes everything in a flash: the student's blonde hair, his spectacles, and the dirty white lab coat that barely fits him. Though they say a great deal about him, nothing speaks louder than his attitude and his words.

"I am frightfully sorry," sputters the young man. "Can I help you?"

Talkative, accommodating, and apologetic. Perfect.

"I am looking for Dr. Craft."

"Well, you have come to the right place." He glances up at the name over the door. Sherlock blushes. The obvious is not always his forte. "I work for him," continues the young man, "or, that is, I have volunteered to help him in my spare time away from studies. A friend and I assist him, actually. The doctor's experiments are most intriguing. My friend is a much better medical sort than me, I am afraid. Is Craft waiting for you? Do you have a card?"

"Uh . . ." says Holmes, "my name is Sherrinford. No, I do not have an appointment."

"I see. Well, I can't leave a chap standing in the hall. I like to find the best in others, so I shall assume you have something of importance to convey to the great doctor."

"Yes, I do. Thank you."

"My name is Stamford, and my friend is named John. You shall view him in a moment, though you may not see him face on, since he is a most assiduous and dedicated chap, much more so than me, and is always bending over his studies and taking notes for Dr. Craft. 'Notes' is not the correct word. He writes veritable stories about our experiments, makes them *so* interesting. Craft just adores him and loves to read his reports."

Stamford opens the big doors. Sherlock is instantly transported into heaven. It is a big room, with white walls, of course, and a very high ceiling. It is filled with wide, low lab tables, and upon them are bottles and torts and test tubes and flaming Bunsen lamps. Liquids all the colors of the rainbow run through clear hoses and rest or simmer in the glass containers. Bubbling and boiling sounds echo in the room. And at the far end, bending over a notepad, doing exactly what his friend Stamford said he would be doing, is the aforementioned John. He looks about Stamford's age, a little portly, with his wide back turned to Holmes.

"John will return here to study to be a doctor one day, mark my words," says Stamford.

"A young man with both sides of his brain fully developed," says Sherlock, almost as much to himself as to Stamford. "What a marvelous companion he must be."

"Excuse me?" says Dr. Craft, who stands at a table halfway down the room. He has turned and noticed Sherlock. "Who are you?" He sounds angry.

Holmes bursts into tears.

Stamford doesn't know what to do. He appears to have allowed someone into the room whom the doctor does not like. And now, this someone is crying uncontrollably. He reaches out to console Sherlock, then pulls back.

"Now, now," says Craft, advancing toward Holmes, "there is no need for that. I didn't mean to startle you, sir." The third man looks up for a second, then turns back to his notes.

"It isn't that," sobs Sherlock, glancing up to observe Craft as the doctor puts a hand on his shoulder. He has short black hair, a goatee, and dark spectacles. His lab coat is sparkling white. *Concerned about his appearance, gruff on the exterior, soft inside, will be susceptible to my particular approach. Excellent!* "I . . . I am merely overcome by being here."

"And why is that?"

"This is where . . ." Sherlock breaks down again.

"Come, man, get a hold of yourself. Speak, and I shall help you with whatever you require."

Holmes glances at him. *A genuine statement, I think. I shall pursue this.* "I am a dear, dear friend of a man named Grimsby."

"Grimsby? That sounds familiar."

"Murdered a few short days ago, horribly murdered."

"Ah, yes, the little one who was killed and thrown into the Thames."

Sherlock convulses in tears again.

"Here, here, nothing can be done about it. What can I do or say to help you? If you take hold of yourself, man, I shall assist you in your grief. You must control your nerves."

"I . . . I just wanted to know how you think it was done. I don't know why I ask that. I have often heard it said that grieving ones always want to know such things. Perhaps it provides some comfort?"

"Well, yes, that appears to be true sometimes, but perhaps not in this case."

Sherlock reaches into his reservoir of acting roles and makes the tears well up again in his eyes. "Why so?"

"We had the body here for just a very short time, but I do recall it as a strange case. I believe he was crushed by some force that wrapped around his midsection. His ribs, on both sides of the cage, were broken from the fourth through the seventh, and at least one of them punctured a lung, in fact both lungs."

"Crushed by a force, did you say?"

"Yes, a force. But that is all I can say. I cannot fathom what it was. It seemed almost . . . inhuman."

"Inhuman?"

"But what creature, about in London, what inhuman force, could have done such a thing? I recall asking myself that question. But the victim was not someone with connections in society, as you know, so we did not pursue it. What can one do? There are so many misfortunes in this city."

To the astonishment of the doctor, the young man asking the questions, so profoundly sad and inconsolable just moments ago, suddenly brightens and shakes his hand vigorously.

"Thank you, sir. You have been most helpful."

And with that, he vanishes from the room, down the stairs, and back out into the streets.

Inhuman force.

It isn't a description that would fit the abilities of some common London thief in a street fight with Grimsby. *But I wager that in some way it fits Crew. And if it doesn't, I can make it. Now, I just have to find him.*

17

WHAT SUTTON KNEW

It takes Sherlock about twenty minutes to cut through the Old City, head toward the river, and reach London Bridge Railway Station on the other side, not far from Snowfields School. Once he has his ticket, he finds his platform but doesn't board his train. Instead, he spends the half hour before it departs walking about the station watching for anyone following him. Then he heads to the wrong platform before darting back to his own and slipping onto the train just as the whistle sounds for final boarding. No one seems to have followed. He is safely on the ten past noon train to Rochester.

They chug off through Southwark and he watches the city from the windows in his fourth-class car – the factories, the rookeries, the working-class homes jammed into each other in the gray day. But he focuses on what he must do. The train passes through Greenwich, then the suburbs, into the eastern villages, on toward the coast. They reach Gravesend near the mouth of the great river and, before he knows it, the locomotive is slowing to enter the Strood Railway Station just across the bridge from Rochester.

He must find Hopkins. It won't be easy. And when he locates him, things might even turn violent. This will be a desperate man. Holmes feels for his horsewhip in his coat sleeve. But he has a better tool than that, one he intends to employ to his utmost this time – his brain.

Sherlock gets out at the Strood Station and crosses over the cast-iron Rochester Bridge on the River Medway. The dun-colored town is on display from here, sitting on the far side of the blue water, its remarkable cathedral and ancient castle rising above the modest homes and businesses. He hears the gulls and smells the North Sea.

Where to start?

He puts himself in Sutton's place. The police would not be paying him to live here. They would have simply let him go with several provisions. Sherlock has made it his business to study all aspects of the criminal and police world and he is well versed in this sort of thing – he knows how it works. This was a deal with the devil Sutton, who put to death the even more despicable Brixton Gang boss, Charon. Sutton would be required by the police to stay out of trouble (or they would be happy to hang him), find honest employment, report his whereabouts on a regular basis, and never ask for their help, whether those who want to kill him are on his trail or not.

Sherlock wishes he could simply have asked Lestrade exactly where to find him. But he couldn't do that to his colleague. It would have put the young detective into a terrible situation if the release of sensitive information were found out. He had said the absolute most that could be asked of him. And anyway, Lestrade might not have known any more than he gave up.

If I had done what Sutton did, where would I go? I would seek employment in a profession that my enemies would never think I would take up, in an office or a store or a place of business where they themselves would never go.

Sherlock runs through the sorts of professions that this might include. Sutton is a clever man and well spoken, remarkably so for a man of his kind, one of the sinister minds behind the many brilliant Brixton Gang crimes. But he has only been free for a short while, not even a year. He hasn't had time to take up a profession that would require training or education, to become a solicitor or a medical man or a clerk of any sort. He would need to seek a lowly job at first, while he plotted his emergence into something more respectable and profitable.

Where would the evil men who pursue him never look for him? Where would they never go?

Holmes is at the final span on the bridge, almost on High Street in Rochester. He stops in his tracks and looks into the town . . . at the famous cathedral.

High Street is a tight artery, jammed with taverns, shops, lodging houses, and other businesses. It is easy to find your way to the cathedral in this town. You simply look up. Sherlock turns right just a couple of streets down, onto College Yard, and approaches the magnificent building. Just a stone's throw from the equally remarkable castle, it rises high in the sky, a light brown, almost white stone gem as big as the giant churches in London. Every English schoolboy knows about the Rochester Cathedral. Sherlock stops for a moment on the expansive green lawn and looks up. It is awe-inspiring, with five spires, the last a massive one, and a huge exterior stained glass window, almost the width of the building, somehow glistening despite the meager sun.

Holmes sees an old man on his knees tending to one of the gardens. *Perfect – a working man who would know another worker.* The big church's clergy might not know of Hopkins if he is doing some menial job here. And it would be better, anyway, not to involve them in his hunt for this devil.

As Holmes pauses near an ornate black bench nearby, the man gets laboriously from his knees, dusts himself off, and enters the cathedral. Sherlock follows. He feels a little guilty about being inside this sacred place, and its quiet beauty overwhelms him for a moment. He stares up.

"Can I 'elp you, young man?"

It is the old fellow he had seen tending to the garden. Holmes was lost in his own head. *I must ask now and seem inconspicuous, just a nobody asking a casual question or two.*

"Y- yes, you may. I am seeking someone, an old friend."

"I shall tell you if I 'ave made 'is acquaintance."

Even their lowered voices echo in the massive church.

"Do you have many new employees here?"

"Is you looking for employment, as well?"

"No."

The man eyes him up and down and seems at first reluctant to say anything more, but then relents.

"New employees is rare 'ere, but –"

"But what?"

Sherlock has cut him off suddenly. The man is taken aback. He looks even more suspicious.

"I was commencing to say that we 'ired one just a number of months back, first new one in all my time 'ere, which runs now about a 'alf century."

"That is impressive, sir, but you were saying?"

"I was saying that we 'ired a new one. To 'elp me, in fact, though I don't need it. It was as if the 'and of God 'ad opened up a job that we didn't 'ave before and gave it to this bloke."

"By the name of Hopkins?"

Mistake.

Sherlock has spoken too quickly. He wasn't able to resist. The man looks at him for a long while.

"'Ow did you know that?"

"Because . . . he is a friend, as I said, and I had heard tell that he had gone out this way and been employed in churchly doings. I thought of the cathedral first, of course."

"You don't say. So, 'e is who you is seeking?"

"Is he here?"

"No." At first, Sherlock thinks the man won't say anything more, but after a pause he continues as if there is something about Hopkins he wants to get off his chest. "'E keeps leisurely hours, does 'e, and the church seems to let 'im. I would not be allowed such liberties."

He doesn't like him. He thinks he's lazy. I'll ask him straight out.

"Do you know where he is?"

"Oh, I can fathom an estimate."

"Which would be?"

"Falstaff's Tavern, eight doors to the east after you turn on High Street."

Hopkins is close by!

Ten minutes later, Sherlock Holmes enters the Falstaff public house. He thinks he looks old enough now to appear to be a patron, not some boy coming to retrieve a father home for a mother. He expects no one to ask him any questions or threaten to throw him out, although what he plans to do once he gets inside and positions himself in the right place will likely end in his being removed rather quickly, or at least secreted into a private booth – he hopes by a particular individual.

On his way back down College Yard and past the eight doors along High Street, he perfected the plan he had formulated on the train. There would be no need for the horsewhip.

The inside of the tavern is much like every old ale house in England, with a low ceiling, dimly lit and full of dark wood, smoke clouding the air, the smell of body odor and beer abounding. It is mid-afternoon and not the loud, public place it will be by nightfall, but far from empty. A man wearing a black bowler jauntily on his head and a woman in a red dress cut low on her chest to show her ample bosom are serving from behind a counter, talking to patrons in a lively manner, and filling their mugs and glasses. A dozen or so others are sitting in the wooden booths that line the walls, mostly two per table. Not one looks to own much more than the pound or two they are spending here.

Sherlock doesn't see the man he seeks at the counter, so he scans the booths. He knows what he is looking for: a man sitting alone, with his back to the wall so he can observe everyone in the tavern and see anyone who comes in or goes out. It is not just the strategy that Bell advises, but the criminal way, built upon living a life of being suspicious of others because you yourself deserve suspicion. Sherlock's eyes rest on a particular man, at the back, of course, hunched over, looking down into his beer, glancing up every now and then to survey others. He wears a heavy coat, though it is warm both inside and out of doors. That is the criminal way too; coats can conceal many things one might need in a moment of desperation. Sherlock eyes him, and it doesn't take long before the look is returned. The man glances away and then glances back, as if he is wondering if he knows this intense, eagle-nosed, black-haired boy in the second-hand frock coat. But the man can't place him. He doesn't like being observed, so he looks down and keeps his eyes on his drink.

But Sherlock can indeed place *him*.

The boy has this man *exactly* where he wants him. He smiles while still looking at his target. The rascal peeks up and sees this. An expression of concern briefly crosses his eyes.

I cannot merely ask him for the information I seek, Sherlock had told himself while looking out of the train window. *He would simply deny that he is who I say he is. He would send me away, threaten me. It is not in his interest to squeal on anyone else, especially the deeply feared Crew. No, I must corner him like the rat he is, in a public place. And then I must make it so he cannot refuse me.* While walking down the street, Holmes had found exactly the right words.

"Is there anyone named HOPKINS here?" Sherlock shouts. The man looks back at him, unsure of what to do. It is unlikely that he has made many friends in Rochester, evidenced by his sitting alone. But he doesn't move. He stays there, not even glancing back. Sherlock is well aware that the mere mention of his assumed name might not move him to action. He can ignore it. But another name will do the trick.

"SUTTON Hopkins?" inquires Sherlock at the top of his lungs.

The man freezes and locks a riveting gaze on Holmes. Without even moving his head, he motions, with his eyes, for Sherlock to come toward him. As the boy does, Sutton rises to his feet and creeps to another booth, deeper in the tavern. Holmes slides in across from him, face to face.

"Who in blazes are you?" whispers the turncoat, leaning forward.

"Someone who knows who you are."

"Evidently. What do you want? I have no money to speak of."

Sherlock spots Sutton's left hand moving inside his coat, and a bulge emerging there in the shape of a knife.

"No need for that," says Holmes.

"If you try to kill me, I will kill you first. They shouldn't have sent a boy for a man's job."

"I am the *man* who put you behind bars, Sutton. And if I had anything to do with it, I would be the *man* who would not only keep you there, but see you hanged."

A look of recognition comes into the criminal's eyes. "Ah, you!" he hisses, examining Holmes. "You are the one, that strange boy, who caught us in Rotherhithe. You have grown." He sits back, a little wary. "I remember the great fire, you with the gun pressed to my head. I really believed you would have killed me that night. You had a lunatic's look in your eye."

"I *would* have killed you. I can be a lunatic when I must. But I am not here to expose you."

"Thank God."

"Unless the need arises."

"What do you mean by that?"

"I need two things from you. Neither involves any injury to you or my telling anyone of any sort that you, coward that you are, live here in disguise."

Though Sutton winces at the word "coward," he looks relieved.

"Ask me, just ask me and I will do it."

"First, you must promise not to tell anyone at Scotland Yard that I was here, that I know of your whereabouts. If you do, I shall return here and shout your name in the town square, the name of Sutton, villainous squeak, thief, and accessory to murder."

The man swallows. "Agreed."

"Secondly, you must tell me where a man named Crew lives."

Sutton swallows much harder. "Crew? No . . . no, not Crew. I can't."

"Yes, you can."

"You seem awfully sure of that. Why should I tell you anything about *him*?"

"Because if you do not I shall do my shouting in the town square here this *very* day, and also announce you in the East End of London in the criminal quarters, and then they will come for you, all those villains who hate you, all those beasts who wouldn't think twice about murdering you in cold blood, in a gruesome way, I should think. Perhaps a man like Crew might do the job himself?"

Even in the dim light of the Falstaff tavern, it isn't hard to detect that all the blood appears to be draining from Sutton's face.

"Answer the question, and I shall leave this tavern and never speak to you or of you again to anyone."

The rat has been cornered. He has no choice.

"We feared Crew more than anyone else, other than Malefactor himself."

The mention of Sherlock's old nemesis, uttered in fear, coming from the lips of one of the most hardened and powerful criminals in London, stops Holmes in his tracks. He can't say a word. He lets Sutton talk.

"It is singular, you know, what Malefactor has done. He gained much of his power as a youth. How did he gather such force in the London underworld?"

"Brilliance," says Sherlock, almost against his will.

"Do you know him?"

"No."

"But you are right. It is brilliance, indeed. I believe he is a genius. He is like a giant invisible spider now, with a web he has spun throughout the criminal world. He is no longer a boy. He is a young man destined for greatness. There is no power like his.".

"He must be stopped."

"No one can do it. No one *will* do it. There would need to arise in London a man of equal genius, of equal bravery, of equal dedication to countering what he is and what he believes in. There would need to be a sword of justice more deadly than his great weapon of evil. There will never be a man like that."

Sherlock Holmes says nothing. He merely sets his jaw tightly.

"Malefactor is –" begins Sutton.

"Tell me about Crew!" spits Sherlock, almost shouting.

The turncoat looks alarmed. When he speaks, he is barely audible, as if begging Sherlock to talk softly too. "Even Charon feared him. Even Charon! Crew is Malefactor's main one, you know. Grimsby is just for show, a little fellow who will do anything he is asked and can be used."

"Grimsby is dead."

"Dead?"

"Murdered in a most vicious manner and thrown into the Thames. He crossed Malefactor. I spoke to the doctor who examined his body. He said that what was done to him was inhuman." Sherlock stares off into the distance.

"How do you know this?" The man almost gets up. "Who are you, really? Are you with the –"

"Never mind who I am."

"I –"

"Someday you will know. Everyone will know," snarls Sherlock Holmes.

Sutton doesn't like the look on the young man's face. The lunatic in him has returned. His gray eyes seem to have turned black. They stare out at nothing.

"Grimsby crossed Malefactor? Then it must have been Crew who killed him."

"Yes," says Sherlock, nodding to himself.

"He did it as surely as we are sitting here." Sutton actually looks afraid. "It was inhuman? Is that what you said? I . . . I cannot tell you anything more, not a single word."

"You must," says Sherlock. He grins at his listener.

"Well, I don't know where he lives."

"I believe you."

"You do?"

It doesn't make sense for Sutton to hide anything. He knows I will expose him if I am not satisfied, or that I will come back for him if he gives me an answer I find to be false. It is in his interest to tell me the truth. I will make him tell me what he knows. And I will use it.

"I will tell you what I know."

"I have every confidence in that. Begin."

Sutton had known that night in Rotherhithe a few years ago that this was a unique boy, but now, as he sits here with him, cleverly cornered by him, bested at every turn in their dealings, and becoming aware that he knows things that someone of his age and experience has no right to know, he is aware that this young man is even more than he first thought, unlike anyone he has ever met. It is as if this young genius can look at him, examine him, and know his very thoughts. It is in his best interest to spill every bean in his jar.

"Crew is a very unpleasant human being. There is something wrong with him, something not right in his brain. He is ill up there. If you have ever been in his presence, you will know that he seldom speaks."

Sherlock thinks again that he actually knows almost nothing about Crew. Though reading others by their appearance is a specialty of his and he has honed that skill more and more over the years, for some reason he has never tried it on Crew. Perhaps there is nothing to read. The big, fat boy with that little brush mustache and the straight blonde hair parted way over on one side and hanging down over his forehead is like a blank slate, quiet by Malefactor's side every time Sherlock has been with them, allowing his boss and the talkative little Grimsby to take center stage. He has only heard his voice once or twice – high-pitched and nasal, uttering just a few syllables, his blue eyes dead even when he speaks.

"The word among the few who know anything of Crew is that he came from a military family. That upbringing is still there in the way his hair is shaved up so high on the back of his neck. His father believed that affection was not for boys. Crew was rarely touched as a child, not even by his mother, that's what the street says. There was never any tenderness. He grew to hate his father and murdered both his parents, horribly and effectively. He escaped prosecution.

Malefactor was intrigued. He investigated the celebrated crime and collected evidence that proved the identity of the murderer. Then he brought Crew into his employ with the threat of exposing his despicable deed. But soon he discovered that Crew was happy to be with him, anxious to commit whatever atrocities were required, simply in need of a brutal leader to tell him what to do. It is a perfect marriage. If Malefactor wants you dead, you will be, silently and viciously, and Crew will do it."

Sherlock thinks of Malefactor's threats in the apothecary shop and feels a little faint.

"Crew is incapable of affection of any sort," continues Hopkins. "It is certain that he lives alone and has no friends. He hates many people and things. He hated Grimsby, for sure, and hates even Malefactor, though his loyalty to his boss is unswerving. He also hates animals – it is said that he kills them for amusement. He doesn't like anyone who isn't English. He hates the Germans, the Dutch, the Irish, especially the black Africans, and, of course, the Jews."

Sherlock winces.

"There is only one thing that he loves."

"What is that?"

"The dead, human dead. He has been seen lingering over bodies after he kills, fascinated by corpses, the human shell with the life and spirit gone from it. It is said that he likes to talk to the dead too. Someone once heard him screaming at his father."

"Can you, at least, harbor a guess," asks Sherlock in a shaky voice, "about his residence?"

"I have never spoken to anyone who knows where he lives. I am sure that is by design. We all know not to follow him. We know that if we ever tried, that would be the last thing we did. But I do know this: he is often seen crossing London Bridge heading south late at night. Crew does not like to walk. He does not like exercise of any sort. So, one would guess that wherever he lives is just over the bridge in Southwark."

That is both good and bad news for Holmes. Bad because the mad and brutal Crew obviously lives close to his school and not far from Beatrice, but good because Grimsby's body was thrown into the Thames not far from there, making the chance that Crew committed this crime and could be made a suspect and perhaps convicted a better possibility.

"I take it that you have seen him crossing the bridge?"

"Yes, I have."

"Can you tell me anything about that? You are schooled in examining others. Is there ever anything in his dress, his person, his attitude, that might indicate where he is going?"

"Nothing. He is an empty human being. He has no character. There is only evil in him."

"Does he ever carry anything? Does he buy a meal anywhere and bring it with him?"

"He sometimes has a sack. But I don't think it contains food."

"Why do you say that?"

"They are always thick canvas sacks, usually large, sometimes so large he can barely handle them, and there is often something moving inside them."

"Moving?"

"Squirming, writhing."

Sherlock swallows. "What could that be?"

"I am loath to guess."

"Anything else?"

Sutton wants to do all he can to help this brilliant young man. The more he can give him, the more satisfied he will be. He is no fool and knows he must please his inquisitor. Only that will keep him safe.

"I feel I misspoke when I said that he hates animals. He doesn't hate them all. There are stories that he buys exotic creatures. No one knows what, though many say they are of the lethal sort. Everything I know about Crew has been told to me. I never ask questions about him. So, I have never enquired further."

An idea has come into Sherlock's brain. He immediately gets to his feet.

"That is all I need from you." He turns to go.

"You," says Sutton, "you won't tell them, will you? You won't tell anyone?"

"I am a man of my word."

"I thank you for that. Might I shake your hand?"

Sherlock looks at the extended hand as if it were a cloven hoof. "You, sir, are on the wrong side." He walks briskly from the tavern.

All the way back to London on the train he tries to concentrate on the next part of his plan. But it is difficult to do. He had always known that Crew was a dangerous fellow, but the fear he saw in the eyes of the men in the sewers and in Sutton is alarming. Would it not be beyond dangerous to pursue Crew? Would it not be almost suicidal? No one dares, not even the toughest and most evil of London's criminals.

Should I?

But he can't resist the opportunity that is before him. Grimsby is dead; Crew can be fingered as his murderer, and perhaps Malefactor as the man who commissioned the deed. This chance may never come again.

I can wipe out the heart of evil in London. I, Sherlock Holmes. I can destroy all of them.

18

SCUTTLEBUTT

The next morning, after meticulously informing Sigerson Bell of his intentions, Sherlock makes his way southwest to the Cremorne Gardens. It was here that he did much of his investigating while pursuing the magicians last year during the Hemsworth-Nottingham dragon case. He is hoping that a certain someone still resides in the park.

"Master Sherlock 'olmes, under-the-covers man for Scottish Yard, agent of great renown, is that you?"

Scuttle is lying on the ground, half in and half out of his overturned old dustbin. He was fast asleep when Sherlock roused him with a slight tap of his boot to a shoulder. He is still focusing his eyes.

"It is me, sir. How are you keeping?"

Scuttle gets up to a sitting position.

"It is pleasurable to see you. Scuttle is tolerably fit. I 'ave been taking to the exercising of my brains and the thinking more of my muscles. Mr. Starr, 'e the king and president of the World's End 'otel, whom the acquaintance of whom you made, is giving me more occupations. 'E is threatening to deliver up to Scuttle an abode in the 'otel in the basement where 'e will feed my mouth more victuals to make my insides more 'appy, in exchange for more work from Scuttle."

"I am glad to hear it."

"So is Scuttle."

"Do you still note the famous people who frequent this area? Do you still speak with them? I remember being impressed by the folks you encountered."

"Well, they wants to speak with Scuttle, no doubt, but I shuns them now. I do not even look at the papers anymore, at the illustrious-stations. I 'ave learned that most celebrant-ites are not people of substances. Famousness isn't of value unless substances are involved."

"You don't say?"

"I do say. In fact, I 'old forward, I oral ate. This very week, the Queen wanted to speak with me again!"

"The Queen?"

"And I said no. Florence Nightingale too."

"Actually, Master Scuttle, the Queen *is* a woman of substance, and so is Miss Nightingale, real substance. You could have spoken with them."

"I could 'ave?"

"Indeed."

"Well, I did not. I even turned Mr. Dickens down, just yesterday."

"Uh, Scuttle?"

"Yes, sir?"

"Mr. Dickens is dead. He was dead yesterday too, as dead as a doornail."

Scuttle somehow turns whiter than his regular complexion. "Mr. Dickens is dead? Then who will speak up for us?" A tear comes to his eye and runs down his cheek. He wipes at it so aggressively that he seems to be tearing it from his face. "Never mind! It may not 'ave been him Scuttle conversated with. It was, no doubt, in short, some sensationalist novelist, and I shunned him! Magnificantly!"

"Good for you. What about His Highness Hemsworth, the great magician? Have you seen him nearby lately?"

Sherlock had brilliantly caught the red-haired Hemsworth and the Wizard of Nottingham in the attempted murder of His Highness's former wife some ten months ago. But they had eluded that serious charge, been convicted of a lesser one, and served only brief jail terms. Just a few weeks past, they had gained their freedom. Now they were using their notoriety to debut a series of sold-out shows in a West End theater.

"I have no interests in such a parsonage," says the disgusted little boy. "'E is a bad man. Scuttle is ashamed that 'e took any noticing of 'im before. All of London should be em-bare-assed! But I 'ears that the Sunday papers were of great interest in 'im after 'e and Notting'am did their terrible deeds of intentional murder and napping kids. I 'ears that the papers were aroused too when the villains were ejaculated from prison, and sent many men to cover them up in their columns and pillars."

Sherlock can barely follow him, but it doesn't matter. He is edging him toward the point of this little interview.

"You are in and out of the hotel, my friend, so you can tell me this. It is of extreme importance to Scotland Yard. Is

Hemsworth still operating his den of magical tricks and strange animals in the space under it?"

"I shall impregnate you with this information, for Scottish Yard. It is with much sorrow that I say that I 'ave spied him, yes, comings and goings from 'ere these last few weeks since 'e was ejaculated from behind bars."

"Do you know if he still keeps the animals?"

"I do."

"And?"

"Yes."

"How do you know that?"

"'E carries sacks at times, when 'e intrudes the premises late at night, some of them very gigantic, indeed, with things squirming in their innards."

Sherlock Holmes absolutely hates to do this. But he must.

He has offered his card, his homemade card, at the box office of the Egyptian Hall theater. Hemsworth and Nottingham's show has just opened here. He knows they will be rehearsing in the hall this very afternoon. The show is still working out its imperfections, though it is currently the biggest thing on the London stage. The woman in the box office takes the boy's card and slips through the doors leading into the main hall. She returns in seconds, motioning for him to come forward.

"Ah! Sherlock Holmes!" says Hemsworth in his big voice the instant the boy is ushered down the aisle. The magician's hair and goatee are glistening with oil even in the afternoon. His face, as always, looks false. Nottingham, his darker hair in a similar style, is sitting on a guillotine at the back of the stage, smiling too. "What can I do for you? It is so lovely to see you!"

"I have one question, and then I will leave."

"Would you like an admission for the show? You know, though we have had our disagreements, I admire you, your prodigious brains. We are alike in some ways."

"We are nothing alike," spits Sherlock. "Are you still purchasing and importing exotic animals?"

"Like a dragon, for example?" Nottingham lets out a roar from behind.

"Like things in sacks that squirm."

Both the magicians are silenced by this.

"That is a secret thing, which few know. You astound me, Holmes. And just for that, just in admiration, I shall answer you. It seems you know a great deal anyway. Yes, I am still importing. In fact, I did so from behind bars. And the things in bags that squirm, they would be . . . snakes."

"Snakes?" says Sherlock, his voice breaking.

"I see a little fear in your eyes, Holmes. Not a fan of snakes? You don't like the world's biggest constrictors, the Orient's most frightening pythons, the earth's most poisonous vipers?"

"Is that what you acquire?"

"Perhaps."

"And transport in sacks?"

"Perhaps."

"Do you have a client named Crew?"

"Doesn't ring a bell."

Crew would never give his real name.

"A silent fellow with dead blue eyes, combed-over straight blonde hair, a narrow brush mustache, big and slightly pudgy?"

Sherlock sees a flash of recognition on Hemsworth's face, but he moves instantly to hide it.

"My clients' names are no one's business but mine."

"And yet, you just told me," says Holmes with a smile.

He doesn't look back as he leaves the theater, but his grin doesn't lessen. It is wonderful to read the face of a magician, especially this one.

19

AMONG THE DEAD

"Let me see," says Sherlock to himself in his bed in his wardrobe that night. "Crew travels over London Bridge in the dark, sometimes carrying snakes in sacks. What is just over the bridge?" He knows the area well. He crosses over that very viaduct on a regular basis. (The fact that this fiend may live in the same area where he goes to school still gives him pause.) "What is there? Well, right where it reaches land you would find London Bridge Railway Station, St. Thomas's Hospital, and St. Saviour's big cathedral." Wellington Street meets the bridge on the south side of the river and then becomes Borough High Street. The Holmes family once lived near there, above the Leckies' hatter shop, near the rookeries of the rough district known as the Mint. Off High Street, all the neighborhoods are tough and poor. Where, exactly, might Crew be? Again, Sherlock considers the idea that because Crew doesn't like exercise and yet seems to walk home each night, he must live near the bridge. Holmes can't sleep and stays up for a while, sitting cross-legged, concentrating. Nothing makes sense to him. He lies down again and drifts off.

A horrible nightmare comes to him. Malefactor, Grimsby, and Crew are chasing him over London Bridge. He has a revolver and is shooting back at them as he runs. He knows he cannot escape unless he destroys them. One of his shots hits Grimsby in the chest. The little man shrieks. It is a heartbreaking cry, and when Sherlock glances back, he sees the villain lying on the stone foot pavement of the bridge in a piteous mess, very still. Guilt so overwhelms him that he halts and almost lets the others catch him. But he gathers himself and runs again. Malefactor stops and points a finger at him, ordering Crew to run him down and murder him, then rises into the sky, his face becoming the entire dark dome over London. He looks down upon Sherlock, immortal. Crew, his face impassive, gains on him with each stride. Holmes feels that he will be safe if he can just reach the other side. But London Bridge becomes incalculably long, never ending. Crew moves with inhuman speed and catches him. Sherlock is squeezed in an iron grip until he expires, his life and spirit forced out of him as the air is expelled from his lungs. Despite lying dead on the stones, Sherlock can still see Crew's face. The villain's hair hangs down over his victim, its strands hissing, rattling, and darting. There is a look of great curiosity in Crew's blue eyes now, a smile of intrigue below his brush mustache. He is examining Sherlock, fascinated for one simple reason: because he is dead.

Holmes awakes with a start. It is pitch black in his wardrobe. He suddenly knows where he will look for Crew in the morning.

He spends all of breakfast, as he and Sigerson Bell consume hard-boiled eggs, pickled eggs, and tea, explaining his plans to the last detail. The old man shakes his head.

"You are doing it again, my young knight."

"I don't follow you, sir."

"You are giving away your strategies."

"But you are a confidant, sir, someone upon whom I can bounce my –"

"It worries me."

"Worries you?"

"First of all, what you are planning is alarmingly dangerous."

"One must take chances and be brave in the occupation I intend as my life's work. And –"

"More importantly, I am concerned that I know why you are doing this."

Sherlock gets to his feet.

"I must be going," he says quickly. "I have school today. I shan't be back until very late. Please don't wait up."

"But you are not wearing a disguise."

"No." And without another word, he is out the door.

Bell goes to the latticed bow windows and watches his charge walk down Denmark Street.

"Could it be true?"

When school ends that day, Sherlock doesn't cross back over London Bridge to the City and home. Instead, he stays in Southwark and walks up wide Borough High Street to a public house he knows not far from his old neighborhood in the Mint and orders a slice of steak and kidney pie and a small mug of ale. He sits in a booth and takes his time eating. To anyone watching, he would seem like a relaxed young man in a slightly tattered, barely respectable, second-hand frock coat, minding his own business, nothing more in his thoughts than his day's undertakings and whatever leisure activity he might be planning for the evening. But Sherlock Holmes is moiling inside. He is wondering if he should get up and go home as fast as his legs can carry him. He thinks of what Sutton said about Crew. In the past, Holmes has confronted Grimsby several times, been in mortal combat with him on the cobblestones of London alleyways. But never Crew. That thug only once laid a hand on him, and then merely to hold him so Grimsby could strike. If Crew had ever truly attacked him, Sherlock now realizes, *I wouldn't be sitting here today, enjoying this pie.* And yet, Holmes is about to do what no criminal in London has ever dared – he is about to seek Malefactor's disturbed young lieutenant in the night and try to trace him to his lair.

When he gets to his feet, his legs are shaking. But he forces them forward and steps out into the street. In five minutes, he is back near the bridge. He doesn't wait on its stone surface, against its balustrades, its stone staircases, or even anywhere on Wellington Street, where the bridge meets the banks of the Thames. Instead, he takes the steps that lead down off the west side of the street onto the grounds of St. Saviour's Church, the magnificent, towering cathedral that sits there near the water.

Ever since he heard about Crew's fascination with the dead, especially since his frightening dream, Sherlock has been considering that disturbing obsession. When he arose this morning, it was paramount in his thoughts. And, instantly, he thought of this church, rising here just over the bridge with its green, wooded cemetery to the south. Underneath this big edifice, he has often heard it said, rests a huge, underground crypt. It is filled with coffins, with the massive cathedral's many centuries of dead.

St. Saviour's is the oldest Gothic church in London, built five or six hundred years ago. It plays that role well. Almost beige during the day, it grows dark at night, its many ornate points and turrets making it seem like a haunted medieval shrine against the black London sky, its angled stone faces and stained-glass windows lit ghoulishly by gaslights and candles.

Sherlock finds a spot near the castle-like front doors and lowers himself behind the big stone steps, making sure he is out of sight but still has a view of the bridge and the entrance to the church grounds from Wellington Street. He will be able to spot anyone who comes this way, but they will not be able to see him. He can still smell the Thames from here. This is a creepy place. To his left is Clink Street, where the city's famous old prison was, just a stone's throw from where the ancient bear-baiting arenas were, where Shakespeare's Globe Theatre used to be and its bohemian actors lived. The Marshalsea Prison, where Charles Dickens's father was held as a debtor, is nearby too. This church and its grounds are like an island, a refuge in a sea of frightening legends. One hears strange sounds in the night.

He pulls a copy of the latest installment of *The Mystery of Edwin Drood* from his frock-coat pocket: June issue, chapters ten to twelve. Sigerson Bell had been spending the shilling each number cost right up until Mr. Dickens died. The great writer had been sitting at his desk, plotting and imagining this mystery, his first real work of crime fiction, until the very hour before his passing. The novel, a tale of murder (it seems) near or in the Cloisterham Cathedral, complete with its crypt and lime pit, has been riveting both Sherlock and his master. They have been reading it aloud to each other, Sherlock with some restraint and Bell with great flourishes of drama. But now this story of such great intrigue will never be completed. No one will ever know, for sure, who murdered Edwin Drood, or if he simply vanished into thin air. There are those who think they have the answers, but to estimate and understand the imagination of Charles Dickens, to think you could even begin to know the twists and turns that might have ensued is, to Holmes, a gross assumption bordering on the absurd. Upon the news of Dickens's death, the old apothecary had wept uncontrollably. Sherlock had thought it was as much for the loss of the conclusion to this fascinating story as it was for the passing of the great figure himself. There will be a few more installments published, as if written by a dead man.

Sherlock brought these chapters with him because he knew he would need not only something to do while he waited, but something that could truly divert him. He intends to raise his head at the end of every paragraph, so he can both stay on his toes as a lookout and keep his fear under control, his imagination not flirting with the horrible things that Crew might do to him, but instead on the marvelous murder mystery.

But it is hard going. Even Dickens cannot keep him from the terror that he has been fighting to control all day. As well, Cloisterham Cathedral, its crypt and its lime pit, scare him, especially as he crouches here in the night near another cathedral, renowned for its dead room. And the villainous character John Jasper frightens him too. Though Jasper has a dark complexion, Sherlock keeps imagining that his face looks exactly like Crew's.

Eventually, he is compelled to raise his head and rivet his gaze on the entrance to the church grounds near the bridge. The sun sets, the sky grows dark, and a thick foggy, humid night descends. He hears the crows calling from vantage points on the cathedral and turns and looks up at them for a moment. The dark building looms above him, truly like a haunted place, with that crypt below.

When he glances back toward the bridge, he just catches the top of a bulbous blonde head descending the stairs to the church grounds. A huge sack is slung over the figure's shoulder.

With his heart leaping, Sherlock jumps to his feet and clumsily stuffs *The Mystery of Edwin Drood* back into his coat pocket. It takes him a moment, and when he looks back, Crew is gone. He can't even spot him through the trees on the walkway at the bottom of the stairs! The fiend is on the grounds somewhere, and Sherlock has lost sight of him! There couldn't be anything worse. The huge church, with its nooks and crannies, its dark surfaces, and its treed lawn and cemetery, is perfect for sneaking up on a victim. It is deserted at this hour too. The bridge, on the other hand, and Wellington Street and Borough High Street beyond are still crowded. The noise of the carriages and the shouts of people and the horns on the boats on the black river provide a perfect sound barrage to muffle any screams in the night.

I must get out of here! But if I move, if I take my back from the wall behind me, I will be even more vulnerable. Does he know I am here? Has he spied me and then slipped onto the grounds to kill me? What, exactly, is in that sack tonight?

He hears footsteps coming toward him.

20

CREW'S LAIR

Sherlock tries to make himself small, even smaller than Grimsby. He curls into a ball and presses himself against the stone wall, back from the stairs. The footsteps come closer, and then stop. Whoever is there is standing next to the bottom step, no more than twenty feet away. Holmes can hear that person breathing. It is labored, like someone winded merely from walking. More than a minute passes; the heavy breathing continues, and its author remains still.

Sherlock can't stand it. He needs to know if it is Crew. He raises his head slightly, until he can see through the little openings in the balustrade that serves as a stone railing for the stairs.

Crew is peering back at him!

Can he see me?

Then something diverts the thug's attention, as if he were jolted by an unseen force. Even from where he is, Sherlock can tell that the source of the disturbance is the sack that the villain carries over his shoulder. And Holmes can now see that that sack is enormous.

"Settle, my pretty," whimpers Crew in his high-pitched

whine, "settle." He drops the sack down and pets and kisses it. Sherlock can see the shape of giant coils inside. "We are almost there, almost." And with that, Crew forgets about looking toward Holmes's hiding place and heads around the church in the direction of the cemetery on the south side.

The boy waits until the fiend is out of sight before he rises. He realizes that he is sweating profusely. The smart thing to do would be to go the other way, up those steps toward London Bridge and home. That's what others would do.

That's why he doesn't.

He sees his mother's dead face in his imagination. He sees Angela Stonefield's deformed monster head with her beautiful blue eyes staring out at him, lifeless on the basement floor of that little row house in Hounslow.

No one else would follow Crew tonight. No one else ever will. That's why he must.

But he does so carefully. He has indeed chosen not to wear a disguise. If there is someone tailing him, a particular follower, he welcomes him. It will fit into his plan. Still, the very idea frightens him, and he keeps looking around. But curiously, there doesn't seem to be a pursuer of any sort. In fact, he hasn't sensed that anyone has been watching him since he left the school. Perhaps it was expected that he would go home and start from there?

Sherlock rounds the staircase knowing full well that Crew could leap out at him at any moment. *I am shadowing someone who has never been successfully tracked.*

Holmes can't locate his prey, so he ventures farther out until he is far enough along the stone walkway that leads up to the stairs so he can see around the church to the dark graveyard to the south. It is hard to make out anything. The area is well treed, and under the trees tombstones stick up like dark mushrooms upon grass that looks like a placid gray lake in the night.

Sherlock sees shadows amongst the stones, but none take the shape of a man.

But then he sees him, far down the cemetery, almost at the end of it, struggling with his sack. Whatever is inside looks like it weighs as much as a human being. Holmes realizes that he may be in luck (if that is possible, given what he is doing). Crew is preoccupied with his load. He is likely rarely so distracted. This may be the one night he can be tracked.

As Holmes watches, Crew struggles to the end of the graveyard, steps out onto Church Street on the other side, and vanishes. With that, Sherlock's plans go out the window and danger increases. He had believed that Crew was living somewhere on the church grounds, perhaps in this cemetery, or even in the crypt below the building. But Crew has passed through the church property and the graveyard without pause. Sherlock had studied the church and its cemetery on a map.

He knows it isn't a good idea to abandon carefully devised plans when you are in a dangerous situation, especially when you are on the trail of, and in close proximity to, a ruthless fiend who means you grievous harm. If he follows Crew now, he will be doing so without any idea of where he is going, without any forethought about how he might watch him or deal with him should things get out of hand.

But Sherlock decides to be bold. Usually, he isn't a gambler. He believes in scientific approaches to his problems and placing the odds in his favor; both his father and Sigerson Bell have taught him that. But he is about to take a terrible chance. He is gambling that Crew isn't paying attention tonight.

He runs through the graveyard and emerges onto Church Street. Rather than being in a dark, treed area or in a hiding spot around the church, he is now out on the gaslit streets with his murderous enemy. When he gets there, he spots him, continuing to struggle with his sack and not looking back, turning right onto Rochester Street. There are few folks about on these back roads at this hour, mostly poverty-stricken locals, prostitutes, and others who have nothing to lose in life. This isn't a part of London where a regular citizen wants to be during the night.

Sherlock suddenly realizes something, and it gives him an unpleasant sensation in the pit of his stomach. Crew is heading in the direction of the Mint! He is within four or five streets of his family's old flat, above the Leckies' hatter shop where Beatrice still lives with her ailing father.

What is he doing here? Where is he going? Is he drawing me in this direction?

He remembers how Beatrice had betrayed him during the Spring Heeled Jack affair. *Trust no one.*

But a minute later, when he sees Crew turn down Redcross Street, another possibility comes to his mind, and it is more frightening than *anything* he has been considering – it makes his knees shake. But it seems almost impossible. *No human being could possibly live there.*

He is thinking of another home for the dead, directly in Crew's path. It is only two or three minutes away, between the hatter's shop and where he is now. It is known as the Cross Bones Graveyard.

The year before Sherlock was born, it had been closed because it had become the dumping ground for so many rotting corpses. It is fenced off now and abandoned. When he was growing up, he was told to stay away from it. Only the bravest boys played nearby, competing at skittles with the yard's human skulls and bones that had found their way into the streets. Some of those children, it was said, disappeared. Local stories told of this place being many centuries old, originally a spot where prostitutes were buried and later a pauper's cemetery where those so poor that they couldn't afford a funeral of any sort were slung into shallow graves, often one on top of another. When Sherlock was little, its odor could be smelled from a great distance. That stench, the last time he had smelled it, perhaps two years ago, had subsided a little. But it remained a place where few dared to go. It wasn't very large, just a small town block, and most of its trees were dead. It was a place of curses and evil.

Is Crew really going there? And if he is, dare I follow?

Sherlock watches him walking down Redcross Street, keeping far behind, alert for anyone who might be trailing both of them. The buildings are brick and grimy here, tight to the narrow foot pavements on the narrow street. Before long, the gates and walls of Cross Bones come into view ahead of the villain, just north of Union Street and St. Saviour's Parochial School. Crew stops, sets down his sack, and looks back.

Sherlock ducks into a doorway. As he does, someone screams. He looks down. An old woman is lying there, no shoes on her feet, her toes black, without nails. Her dress is the color of dirt and barely covers her. Her hair hangs in strings from her brown-stained bonnet. She has no teeth and smells of some sort of disgusting alcoholic or medicinal brew. Sherlock has stepped on her thigh. But once she has finished screaming, a short cry that pierces Holmes to the heart and has him envisioning Crew rushing down the street toward them, she looks up to see the interesting young man in the old black frock coat. To her, he looks frightened, and not just because she has screamed. She thinks he is trying very hard to seem older than he is. She smiles and reaches out for him. He jumps into the road. The instant he does, he realizes his mistake. He is in plain view. But when he looks up Redcross toward Cross Bones, Crew isn't running toward him.

In fact, the devil is nowhere to be seen.

It takes Holmes more than fifteen minutes to get from where he encountered the old woman to the rusty gates of Cross Bones Graveyard, even though it is no more than two hundred feet away. He moves up the street as cautiously as if he were being hunted, slipping in and out of doorways, looking every which way, even up above, trying to keep himself calm. *Is this a trap?* He can't go back. That would leave him equally open to detection. There is almost no one in the street – just the odd barely clothed woman passes, sometimes followed by a rough man or two. Crew can pounce on him here and murder him in an instant. He thinks of Sutton saying that this enemy enjoys killing in gruesome ways. Sherlock tries not to imagine any of them.

At the gates, he peers through the bars and surveys the yard. In all his years growing up nearby, he had never done such a thing. He never would have dreamed of it. The boys who played with the Cross Bones' remnants never entered. Only the ones who disappeared were said to have actually gone in.

DO NOT ENTER reads a sign above the gates, accompanied by a Southwark seal and another from the Lord Mayor of London.

But Sherlock Holmes is nearly a man now, and he has a sacred quest. He cannot allow anything to stop him, not even the Devil himself. That vow is filling him with courage, though it doesn't still his pounding heart.

As he looks through the bars, he can see that there aren't many tombstones in Cross Bones Graveyard. There are bushes and dying trees and a few overturned markers and little crosses lying on their backs. The ground is rough and stony, disturbed throughout, where corpses were hurriedly buried for hundreds of years, back even before Shakespeare's day. Holmes can smell Cross Bones tonight. He thinks he can see what look like big round stones and sticks everywhere. But he knows that that isn't what they are; they are human remains.

He climbs up on the gate, his whole body shaking. But before he jumps down, he sees something. There's a little building in the center of the yard. It is obscured from view from outside the gates, but can be seen from up here. There are bushes all around it. It isn't very tall, just slightly higher than the average human being, but it is built in the style of a classical structure, white and with the appearance of marble like a Greek or Roman mausoleum, lined with pillars.

A crypt.

And at the front door of that home for the dead, Sherlock now sees Crew. He must have taken his time coming through the graveyard, perhaps looking at the skulls and bones, likely something he enjoys each night. He has set his big sack down. It writhes at his feet. His back is to Holmes and he is working away at the door, probably trying to put a key into the lock in the keyhole, while keeping his foot on the sack so it won't slither away.

Sherlock is so shocked that his foot slips. The top of the gate is lined with the tips of spears. As the boy falls, one of the sharp points enters his throat. Blood spurts from him and he cries out. As he does, Crew turns.

Holmes pulls himself off, falls from the gate, and lands with a thud on the ground outside the graveyard. His throat is sliced near his jugular vein. He staggers to his feet, stopping his wound with a hand. He glances through the bars and sees Crew emerging out of the bushes and coming toward him at a fast walk, looking angry. The sack is over his shoulder.

Though feeling faint, Sherlock takes to his heels. He knows his way around this area and gets to Borough High Street in a flash. From there he sprints to the bridge, flies across it, through the Old City, along Fleet Street, north through Trafalgar Square and all the way back to the apothecary shop on Denmark Street. He loses a great deal of blood, and by the time he is in the door, collapses on the floor, Sigerson Bell by his side in an instant, working to stem the flow from his throat.

Before Holmes had even reached Borough High Street, Crew had arrived at the graveyard gates. There, he found a thick streak of fresh blood on one of the rusty spears. Holding back the writhing sack, he put one of his sweaty, fat fingers to the red liquid and then brought it to his lips. It tasted good. He nodded to himself and smiled.

21

FAREWELL

Sherlock wakes with one thing on his mind. He must see Irene. Feeling vulnerable and mortal, aware that he not only almost died the night before but that he must go back to Cross Bones tonight, enter that crypt, find Crew, and gamble his life again, he dearly wants to see her. It may very well be for the last time, whatever happens. He wonders if an opportunity lies before him – to set aside all this manly nonsense about fighting evil for the rest of his life and take the young woman he really loves into his arms and go with her wherever she goes, live a normal *and* exciting life with the beautiful Irene. But what would she say?

"My boy!" exclaims Sigerson Bell, though it sounds little like an exclamation. The old man is leaning over his apprentice in the wardrobe, face inches from him, long stringy hair cascading in little streams down toward his chest, fishy garlic-onion breath wafting out in clouds, spectacles almost falling off his big beak, and a smile on his face. He is fiddling with the wide white bandage he affixed to his young friend's throat, making sure the slimy liquid (made of God knows what – perhaps ground bat wings and owl refuse) is in place. Sherlock is alarmed, but not because of the disturbingly close proximity of this strange man. He adores Sigerson Bell, warts and all (and the apothecary, incidentally, has a number of real warts, the most spectacular being one the size of a walnut on the back of his neck). Sherlock's alarm arises from the old man's voice. He is very hoarse.

"Your voice," says the boy.

"Just the common cold," replies Bell, but he is unconvincing. When he pulls back from Sherlock and lets the boy get to his feet, he actually has to stagger to get to a stool by the lab table. The old man almost knocks over one of the many stacks of books that line the room. Then he begins to cough. He cannot stop, and the blood comes up in gobs. He has no handkerchief and tries to stem the flow with his shirt-sleeve. It is soon bright red.

"Mr. Bell!" cries Holmes and rushes to him. He puts his arms around him and embraces him while he convulses. He thinks of the day his mother died as he held her in his arms, and starts to cry.

Bell stops coughing. "Cease and desist!" he says to Holmes. "Close your waterworks! I cannot abide it!"

"But sir –"

"Sir, nothing. I am as fit as a fiddle."

"Sir, you are dying."

He has never said it before.

"And what of it? We all die. I may have fifty years left!"

But it is obvious that he has just days, perhaps hours.

"I am more concerned about you, my boy. How is your throat?"

Sherlock realizes that it doesn't even hurt. Whatever Bell has done to his wound has performed a miracle. He is not surprised. He slowly peels back the bandage and looks in the mirror he keeps in his wardrobe. The scar is ugly and a little red but already healing. He doesn't feel "fit as a fiddle," but is well enough for what he must do today.

"I am fine."

"You must sleep another day or two."

"Another?"

"You have been in your bed for nearly forty-eight hours."

Sherlock is shocked. But then they both hear his stomach growl.

"I know a certain calf-brain scone that has your name on it!" cries Bell hoarsely.

Holmes hates to hear that familiar high-pitched voice rendered to this croak. But the apothecary prevails upon him to take his breakfast and makes sure he eats enough for two men. He won't hear of the boy consuming fewer than two flasks of tea. In the midst of the meal, the old man staggers away, somehow climbs up his spiral staircase, and then struggles back down.

He approaches Sherlock from the rear, looking a little sheepish, holding something behind his back.

"I . . . I purchased this for you," he says in a tiny voice, still awfully hoarse. He whips his present around with a flourish, so the boy can see it. He is holding a new suit of clothes and shining black boots. They are fresh from a tailor and cobbler shop. *New!* Sherlock Holmes has never had a single piece of new clothing in his life, and he is someone who is desperate to look respectable, obsessed about a spotless appearance, even when dressed in ragged clothes. The suit is pitch black, well tailored, with a waistcoat and crisp white shirt and necktie. The boots are made of good leather and cut high to go partway up the calf. The boy will look even taller in them. This would have cost Sherlock two years' wages.

"I thought of getting you a deerstalker hat for any trips you might make in your future out into the cold winds in the countryside, but decided against that."

Holmes is speechless. He sees himself in this suit years from now, an elegant man, a private consulting detective in his own rooms in London. But when he pictures it, his employer is not by his side. That's when it hits him: this present is a parting gift. Sigerson Bell has loved him and sheltered him and taught him all the remarkable things he knows, and now he is saying good-bye. He thinks of the tradition in the old man's strange Trismegistus branch of his family, of the father purchasing a suit for his son so he will have a fine one to wear to the father's funeral.

When Holmes looks into his master's eyes, he sees tears forming. "Cease and desist!" cries the boy, his own eyes reddening. "Close your waterworks. I cannot abide it!"

They argue about Sherlock's plans for the night. The boy outlines what he intends to do, and it frightens the apothecary. Bell has arranged for his ward to have the next few days off from school and had expected him to spend them quietly at home, mostly in bed recovering from his wound. But it is really the old man who needs rest. He desperately needs it. By the time they near the end of their conversation, he can barely hold his eyes open, and when Sherlock stops speaking, his fading friend falls asleep. Holmes carries Bell up to his bedroom and puts him under the covers, worried as he listens to his heavy breathing.

Sherlock can't stay put. He can't listen to Bell dying. Holding back his emotions (something at which he has been working particularly hard of late), he puts on his new suit and boots, combs his hair fifty times or more, and heads out into the London day, intent upon seeing Irene. He has no idea what he will say to her. But he knows a turning point has come.

After he reaches Montague Street, he spends at least an hour standing next to the British Museum on the far side of the road, working up the courage to see her. There are so many memories attached to that house. He remembers the first time he came here, more than three years ago, when Irene was a sweet and innocent girl who helped her father with his many charities. She and Mr. Doyle had visited him in jail where he was being held on suspicion of involvement in the

Whitechapel murder. When he escaped, he came here. He had been drawn to the house, to her. And she had protected and sheltered him. She had hidden him in the doghouse at night, and they had plotted together during the day in the house's beautiful wood-paneled dining room. Smart and inventive, she had helped him solve the case, but she had nearly died too. It had frightened him to his soul. *Irene can't ever die.* He wonders if pushing her away from his life has been part of what has changed her. She is certainly no longer innocent. She has plans of her own. She is an independent young female, a new woman. *Maybe I shouldn't resent that. Maybe I should just go with her.*

He walks up to the front door and knocks. Mr. Doyle doesn't keep servants. A progressive thinker, he doesn't believe in it. Sherlock hears the yap of a dog. *John Stuart Mill!* He smiles at the thought of that squat little corgi, full of gas.

It is Irene who comes to the door. She is alone, as often is the case at their home – her father is out doing things for others, his new son with him. Miss Doyle is wearing a long, snow-white dressing gown with a high, frilly collar. Her lustrous blonde hair is unpinned, falling down over her shoulders, and she carries a silver brush in her hand. When Sherlock sees her through the glass in the door, she looks as if she were floating. She is an angel, a real and strong-willed one, floating up the hallway toward him.

"Sherlock," she says and actually blushes. He is overjoyed to see that. She looks him up and down, examining his new suit that fits tightly on his long slim frame. "Come in," she says with only a slight hesitation. It isn't something most respectable young women would do, or be allowed to do. But this is Irene Doyle. If she wants to be alone with a young man in her house, she will be.

As she ushers him into the living room, he notices that she isn't wearing shoes. In fact, as he looks closely, he sees flashes of her bare feet under the dressing gown. It makes his heart thump. Her *naked* feet. They are small and so pretty that he can't stop glancing at them. Her gown is pulled tightly around her form and she smells like a rose. She turns with a smile to him as they walk and says, "You look very handsome tonight, *Mister* Holmes."

"So . . . so do you," he stammers, which makes her giggle. "I mean, you look . . ."

"Beautiful? Stunning? Gorgeous? There, you have three choices."

"All of those," he replies. He thinks he can detect, from behind, that her neck colors a little.

"So?" she says when they are seated. She says it with an air of expectation. As he puts his hands on the table, she stretches out hers so they are almost touching. Almost.

John Stuart Mill, now ancient, has been licking Sherlock's pant cuffs as they walk. Now he settles beneath the two of them and offers a little sound that doesn't come from his mouth.

They both laugh. The laughter fades and there is an awkward silence.

"Why are you here, Sherlock?"

"You are leaving soon?"

"Tomorrow, back to New Jersey, then to Paris in the spring."

"For how long?"

"For at least a year, perhaps more, perhaps many years. I may go to Italy too, to Milan." The look on her face is almost pleading. But Irene Doyle has grown too strong, too willful, to ask him directly.

"Many years?"

"Paris and Milan have the best theaters, the best opera houses, the best opportunities for me. It will be so much fun. It would be fun . . . for anyone."

"You know, Mr. Bell has taught me French and Italian."

A look of hope comes to her eyes and she smiles broadly. Sherlock Holmes has never seen anything so beautiful.

"Mr. Bell is a clever man. I am sure you learned quickly."

"I have a facility with languages."

"You have a facility with everything, Sherlock Holmes." She touches his hands.

"Paris would be an exciting place to live," he says.

"Well, you know, there is a great deal of crime there and a great need for detectives, for the best of that lot." She smiles again.

But when she does, she dips her head, a little affectation intended to look slightly shy and irresistible. It is. But it also ends their relationship forever.

As she moves, he sees a scar. It comes out from her hair, the hair she had been combing when he arrived, and snakes across her temple. It is fading now and easily covered when she fixes herself up to go out in public or when she sings on a stage. Sherlock knows where that scar came from – it is slightly more than three years old. It was inflicted upon her by the Whitechapel murderer's horses and coach in High Holborn Street when that villain was attempting to frighten Sherlock away from his trail. *He was trying to murder her, the irreplaceable Irene, my independently and fabulously spirited girl. It was because of me, because of what I did and what I will do!* He sees his mother collapsing in his arms.

Sherlock rises to his feet.

"I . . . I have come to say good-bye." He can barely say it and can't look at her. He turns and marches down the hallway without even touching her. He cannot touch those soft, beautiful hands. If he does, he will never leave her again.

He goes out the door and closes it with a slam. She can feel the passion in that sound. But she sits alone at the table. When she begins to cry, it is in sobs.

Out on the street Sherlock is trying not to think of her. He is concentrating on what he will do to the villainous Crew. *I must seek justice!* But one thought keeps intruding. *There will never be anyone else like Irene Doyle.*

She finally gets to her feet and goes to the door. She opens it and gazes down the street. He is far away, looking handsome even from here in his elegant suit, turning at the front of the British Museum. She isn't sure, but he seems to look back for an instant, and she swears their eyes meet. There is one thought in her mind.

There will never be anyone else like Sherlock Holmes.

But she wipes her tears, sets her jaw tightly, and closes the door.

When we meet again, we will pretend it was a dream.

On the street, the future sword of justice, the scourge of all those with evil intent, sets his jaw tightly too and marches forward.

22

DECISION

Despite the fact that he is going to a graveyard to investigate a crypt and the villain who lives in it, he decides to wear his new suit that night. In fact, he vows to dress much like this, in a suit similar to this one his dear friend has just given him, for the rest of his life. It will be his uniform. One must be respectable. One must always show that one has standards, even when others don't. He makes the necktie into a bow tie and tucks it under his collar, out of the way.

Again, he doesn't care if he is followed. As long as it isn't fatal, it will eventually be helpful.

He carefully combs his hair in the mirror again before he leaves. Bell is in his bed upstairs. He has barely moved all day. Sherlock only checked on him to make sure he was alive. He was, but just barely, breathing heavily.

Holmes is loath to leave him, but he must. He doesn't go until it is dark out of doors. He isn't feeling well either. And it isn't just because of what happened on Montague Street. He has set that aside forever. His wound has begun to hurt again and he feels a little weak. But he must ignore such things. *It is time to strike.*

Sherlock's pace is quick and purposeful until he gets past the cathedral. When he reaches Redcross Street and nears the place where he encountered the old woman, his walk slows, though he isn't conscious of it. As Cross Bones comes into view, he actually stops. Since the day he vowed that he would avenge his mother's murder, he hasn't suffered from a lack of courage in dangerous circumstances. He has always felt driven during the moments when he needed to be brave, often even angry. But as he stands looking at this frightening cemetery and thinks about the perverted personality whom he is seeking inside it, he wavers. Maybe it has something to do with seeing Irene this afternoon. He yearns for her soft embrace and tries to resist it. But when he does, another person comes to his mind. Beatrice Leckie. She lives just three or four streets away.

What if I went to see her?

Almost against his will, he leaves Redcross Street and walks toward the hatter's shop. He will reach it in five minutes. When he moves in this direction, he senses that he isn't being followed. If someone, a particular someone, were tailing him, Sherlock would never go near Beatrice. It is getting late. More than likely, she will be in bed. He tells himself he can just stand outside and look at the shop, his family's old flat above. Perhaps it will give him the courage he needs to do what he must do tonight. As he turns the last corner and heads down their little street with its tiny courtyard, he is still terribly nervous. He needs a friend. He needs more than a friend.

Irene Doyle has always been beyond me. She has her own dreams, anyway. Beatrice is different. She would sacrifice anything for me, anything.

He stops a hundred or more feet away. The shop windows are dark. Up above, the flat is just as black.

That time is gone. Turn around.

But then he hears her. The sound is music to his ears, as musical as his mother's voice. She is laughing. It makes him happy and settles his nervous heart. Then he sees her, emerging around the corner, *out terribly late*, arm-in-arm with her man. It is the same friend he saw her with a few months ago. He is tall and handsome with black hair, dressed as well as Sherlock is tonight, a respectably high top hat on his head. They look at each other, smiling.

At first, Holmes's heart sinks. But then he feels glad too, or at least he tries to. Beatrice Leckie deserves this. *I don't deserve her.* He turns to go.

"Sherlock!" he hears her cry out. Somehow, she has spotted him all the way across the courtyard, as if she could feel his presence. He has half a mind to run, but he turns to her. She suddenly leaves her gentleman, who looks surprised, and comes toward Holmes.

She slows as she reaches him. Her shining black curls descend around her face from her red bonnet. She might not be the loveliest woman in London, she might not be as spectacular as Irene Doyle, but she is lovely to him. She is grown up and ready to move on in her life. There is a pinch of red in her porcelain-white cheeks.

"My," she says as she stops and looks him up and down

and glows at him, "don't you look 'andsome tonight. I feel I should call you *Mister* 'olmes."

"Sherlock will do. You are busy. I should go." He looks off toward the other man, who is walking toward them appearing suspicious.

She glances at him too, then back at Holmes. "No, no, it's nothing. Well, it isn't nothing, but you are 'ere. We 'aven't seen each other for so long. Sherlock . . . were you coming to see me?"

"Yes."

"You were?" She smiles. "I will tell 'im." She flies away, speaks to her companion, who embraces her for a moment then lets her go and tips his hat to Sherlock as he walks away. She rushes back and takes Holmes by the hand.

"Come!" she cries. "Let's go indoors. I want to 'ear why you came 'ere." She sounds excited and puts her hand to her chest momentarily as if to calm herself.

"But, your gentleman?"

"I told 'im we were old friends."

Moments later, he is lighting the fire for her in the shop. They have retired to the living room behind the inner doors. Her ailing father is asleep in his bedroom. Neither of them feels uncomfortable that Sherlock is here, veritably alone with her. They are like family. It feels cozy near the fire. He is glad to be nowhere near that frightening cemetery. When he sits and looks at Beatrice in the big chair across from him, with her bonnet off now and her dress pulled up a little when she sits, which shows her pretty ankles, he feels almost as if he were at home.

Home.

It is an intoxicating thought, almost as addictive as Beatrice herself. Home had been upstairs here. Home had been playing with her as a child. Home is in her beautiful eyes. Their chairs are close together, and she pushes her feet out so they touch Sherlock's.

"Excuse me," she says and giggles, not pulling them back.

"It is wonderful to see you."

"Even more for me to see you. What brings you 'ere so late at night?"

"I can't say."

"That can mean many things. You could be putting it that way because it is 'ard for you to say, because you have something important to relate to me?" She looks at him with anticipation.

"I have missed you."

"Oh, Sherlock." She leans forward.

"I am doing something dangerous tonight. That's why I can't say exactly why I'm in the area."

"Oh." She looks disappointed, sits back, drops her head, and fiddles with the pleats on her plain red dress. "It is a criminal matter, I suppose."

"But I came to see you because I wondered if I should do that dangerous thing . . . or stay here with you."

She sits forward again.

"And what did you decide?"

"That fellow of yours, he seems like a fine gentleman."

"Well, 'e is. 'E 'as good employment, a clerk in the City. 'E is above my station, but 'e doesn't care. 'E wants to marry me, Sherlock." She looks up at him with a pleading expression. "I would not need to work in the service no more. I would be his wife and raise our children, work for causes for the poor and be 'appy." But she doesn't look like she is sure as she peers into Sherlock's eyes.

"Then you should."

"Should I? Should I really?"

"That isn't for me to decide. He is a handsome fellow."

"Yes, 'e is. But who can match you tonight?" she smiles, patting him on the knee.

"You know, Beatrice, when I came near here to pursue this criminal this evening, I was frightened." She takes his hand. Hers feels warm. *Home.* "And I thought, why am I doing this? I should be with Beatrice." He thinks of how comfortable it feels here, how right.

She looks like she might cry with joy. But then she too says something that ends their relationship forever.

"If you were to marry someone like me, and I don't say *me*, but someone *like* me, you could still avenge your mother's death. You could still be what you want to be. We, or two people like us, that is, could live in a nice 'ome. I, or 'oever you married, could work at a job, and I'm sure 'oever you married would be 'appy to work in order to be with the likes of you. I know what you want." She pauses. "You could be a policeman."

Sherlock had been thinking how well she understood him as she began to speak. She was envisioning a future where he could fulfill his destiny. But then she uttered that last word. He stood up.

"I have to go, Beatrice. You stay inside and keep warm. Lock your door. And marry your gentleman. I am very happy for you. You, of all people, deserve happiness."

She doesn't even get to her feet as he leaves the shop. She doesn't even know what she said wrong.

Sherlock walks with purpose out of the shop and into the courtyard. He had almost been seduced by the warmth of her hearth and her heart. He had almost been seduced by true love. He cannot, he can *never*, let that happen. Others may be *policemen.* They can follow the rules and succeed sometimes and not others. They can put a little dent in evil. They can be regulars in that battle. *But not me. I will not play by the rules. I will stab evil in the heart. I will put myself in danger, and villains in much greater peril. I will be Sherlock Holmes.*

He erases Beatrice's kind face from his mind on his way to Cross Bones Graveyard. *I shall live as if I never knew her, never knew Irene . . . never even lived my wretched past.* His heart is pounding again, but not because he is afraid. He is thrilled. He is going to enter the lair of the most dangerous criminal in London.

And he is going to destroy him.

23

INSIDE THE CRYPT

He gets over the fence this time without incident. But when he lands on the other side, he is almost paralyzed with fear. He can literally feel the dead beneath his feet. He forces himself to move forward. While the ground is hard and strewn with rocks and pebbles in most places, it is spongy in others. This makes his toes curl within his new boots. He imagines all the poor souls who are buried here, the prostitutes from centuries ago, the poverty-stricken, and the nobodies. Oh, how horrible it would be to be nobody, to die without even a funeral, to not be memorialized, remembered in any way. He can see the occasional skull and bone and keeps his head up. Here and there he feels that spongy sensation again.

How many layers of bodies are beneath me?

But he cannot allow himself to be preoccupied with such terrors. He must be alert. Crew could appear from behind from anywhere at any second. *He would enjoy murdering me here.* The bushes and trees, many of them dead, block his view of the crypt up ahead, though he sees parts of it, its white marble-like walls shimmering in the moonlight. Sherlock's footfalls seem to strike the ground with great volume, even though he is walking as slowly and gently as he can, his head on a swivel. It is difficult for him to believe that he is actually here. His heart keeps pounding.

He approaches the crypt without being attacked. As he nears, the whole building – which he can see now is circular and about thirty or so feet in diameter and not as tall as he is – comes fully into view. He thinks he can hear sounds coming from inside, though they are faint.

His footfalls seem to resound even louder throughout the quiet graveyard. He moves at a snail's pace, taking forever to come right up to the crypt. When he finally arrives, he can see its thick wooden door, like an entrance to a dungeon. It is sealed shut, likely locked from the inside, and a keyhole is evident.

How do I get in? Should I even try? The evidence is in there. I must.

Sherlock Holmes moves around the circular building, his fingers on the cool surface, feeling it, wondering what to do next. He knows what to look for once he gets inside. *But how in the world do I accomplish that?* He could pick the lock, but he would risk being heard.

As his fingers glide silently along the wall, he feels something unusual. Exploring it more thoroughly, he realizes that it is a hole, about the size of his hand. When he looks down, he sees a slight light coming from it, and when he lowers his face and puts his eye to it, he can see inside the crypt!

What he sees takes his breath away. It is bizarre almost beyond description.

The interior of the building is dug out, so its floor is a good seven feet below ground. Crew is lying on a marble slab that appears to be his bed. He is naked. But he is partially covered up . . . by snakes. Holmes's eyes bulge. There must be at least five of them, big ones, crawling all over the fiend, wrapping themselves around his neck, his midsection, his legs and feet. One even grips his head near his eyes. When Sherlock adjusts his view, he can see four or five more slithering about on the spare marble furniture, hissing and rattling, forked tongues darting out, some pursuing rats the size of small pigs, seizing them to squeeze them to death or bite them with their fangs. There are lizards and frogs too, some convulsing on the floor from snake venom. Crew is on his back, staring up at the ceiling in a sort of frenzy, saying things that Sherlock can't make out. He seems to be talking to them, as if they were pets he is controlling. The snakes are remarkable colors, bright gold and green and black, with ingenious patterns on their skin. They vary in size from little ones no more than a foot or two long to massive cobras of stunning girth and length. One, which he recognizes as an anaconda from an illustration he saw in a book about the Amazon River, is wrapping itself around Crew's chest (to his ecstasy) and looks to be nearly a foot thick. Its length is hard to estimate from where Sherlock watches; much of it is out of sight. It is so big that it seems like some sort of monster from the imagination of a sensation novelist.

Sherlock is reconsidering the idea of entering the crypt. The size and appearance of that giant snake literally staggers him, and he steps back from the hole. When he does, his foot connects with a skull behind him and he falls on it. It explodes beneath him like a gun going off. All that is left of the human being is dust.

Holmes leaps to his feet. *Could Crew have heard that?* He doesn't dare to even put his eye back to the hole. But he doesn't want to run away. Nothing has been proven yet. If he gives up now, all will be lost. He moves around the outside of the crypt, farther away from the hole and the entrance. His breathing becomes louder. It is like a bellows fanning flames.

When he reaches the opposite side of the building, he stops and stands very still. He listens intently for noises in the night. His hands shake as they rest on the crypt's marble exterior. Then he hears something. He listens again. *Footsteps!* He turns in their direction.

But sounds are difficult to locate in this unearthly graveyard. And at that instant, someone comes from the opposite direction and seizes him from behind. Just before he feels a shooting pain in his neck, one that paralyzes him from head to toe, he glimpses Crew's ugly head inches behind his own, breathing on him, uttering little whining sighs. One of his big hands is wrapped around Sherlock's neck. He can feel the villain's heart pounding against his back. It thumps at a disarmingly slow pace, like the beat of a cold-blooded reptile.

Holmes has never been this terrified. But he cannot move, cannot even consider a Bellitsu maneuver. His opponent knows his capabilities and has neutralized them.

Crew begins lugging him back toward the entrance, to take him down into the crypt . . . with the snakes.

24

SATAN AND HIS FRIENDS

Crew seals the door behind them. They descend wide stone stairs into the crypt. It feels hot and muggy inside. Thick webs line the ceiling, spun by spiders the size of fists. There is a fire blazing in a marble hearth, a few tropical plants, and a little pool with thick, putrid water. It smells of snakes and their refuse.

Sherlock cannot move a single muscle. His opponent has his thick fingers on a nerve in his neck that is being squeezed so hard that the effect is paralyzing him. Crew pulls Sherlock over to the marble bed and throws him onto it. Holmes's head cracks against its hard surface. He lies flat and is barely able to look up. When he does, everything is blurry.

"Sherlock Holmes, good fighter," says Crew. He embraces him for a moment, feeling him, caressing his arms with his hands. "Ah," he hisses and slightly smiles. He steps back, still a little cautious, and picks up a small pistol, a derringer, from a marble table near the bed that has legs carved with images of snakes. He trains the gun on Sherlock and walks backward, never taking his eyes from him.

Holmes has only heard him speak once or twice, and even then he had just uttered a few words. The sound of his voice still amazes the boy – high-pitched and whiny, very nasal, so tiny a voice for a big, tough, young man. It is almost childlike. The fiend is hesitant when he talks, as if he understands not only how embarrassing his tone is but also that he is terribly inarticulate. Crew has little interest in communicating with others, so he hasn't cultivated that skill in the least.

"Good fighter," he says again and turns, muttering to himself, "must be careful, keep him down."

He is examining his snakes.

Sherlock manages to raise his head and looks toward them. In a fog, he sees that they are coiled on the floor and around the plants and lounging in the scummy little pond. *He must have pulled them off the bed before he rose and went upstairs to catch me.* He looks at Crew. His sole clothing is a pair of dark trousers, which he must have hastily pulled on. His bare upper body is as white as the marble in the room. There are rings of fat around his middle. His skull is wide in the jaw and narrow in the upper area. There is a blank look on his face.

"Choose one," says Crew to himself, "for Sherlock Holmes."

If this were Grimsby, if he had Holmes at his mercy in this way, he would have been excited beyond description. But Crew looks like a clerk in a bank doing his job. He is choosing a snake to murder Holmes.

Sherlock wanted *most* of this. He wanted to be in Crew's lair so he could see all the snakes. But he hadn't thought he would be lying on this marble bed, woozy and weak, with the slithering creatures between him and Crew, his enemy holding a gun. Holmes cannot get at his target. He cannot apply his Bellitsu or even the horsewhip he has concealed on himself for this night's dangerous assignment.

"Biters?" says Crew as if he were a mere chicken farmer considering the method he might employ to butcher a hen. He scratches his chin, then picks up a long wooden stick with a metal pick on the end and looks at Sherlock with cold eyes that express no emotion. "Eight poisonous biters," he adds, for his victim's information. "First, I present the Black Mamba!"

He points the stick at a frightening green and gray snake more than ten feet long that is emerging out of the scum pond.

"Very deadly, venomous, found in Africa, lovely name." The snake coils around his stick as if in affection for him, but he gently shakes it off.

Holmes watches it, terrified.

"The Sidewinder." Crew points to another snake, a creamy colored little devil no more than two feet long, with brown dots on its back. It had been moving in a bizarre fashion toward Crew, sideways, and now rattles as he indicates it. "From Mojave Desert, symptoms of bite: swelling, nausea, chills, shock, then death." In his growing excitement, Crew is actually stringing together his version of sentences.

He turns to another little one. "Saw-Scaled Viper, from India." As Sherlock looks at it, his mind now numb with fear, it sits at Crew's feet and coils against itself, rubbing its serrated brown scales until they produce a sizzling sound. "Nice noise. Deadly," adds Crew.

A six-foot-long brown and white snake now approaches

him, as if seeking his attention. "Indian Cobra!" he cries, turning to it. It stands up, its neck flaring out in the cobra swell. From where Sherlock lies, the pattern on the back of the neck looks like a pair of eyes and a smiling face. "Venom paralyzes muscles, acts in fifteen minutes."

Crew pivots. "The Boomslang!" he shouts. "Lovely name too!" A four-foot-long snake, a shockingly bright green and black, its skin almost glowing, comes forward. "African," mutters the pudgy fiend. The killer opens its jaws at its master in a massive yawn, its big fangs dripping. "Internal bleeding, then death."

Crew smiles. "Such choices!"

Another snake, at least six feet long, comes up and coils around his foot. "The Puff Adder. Idiots say Swamp Adder. Deadliest snake in Africa! Has killed the most human beings!"

Sherlock is now sweating profusely. He feels like crying. He wants to get to his knees and beg Crew for his life. But he can barely move. The snakes are beginning to hiss together, like an evil choir.

"Most prized biters?" asks Crew as he turns to a horribly huge one. "I present the King Cobra! From the Asian continent." *It is at least fifteen feet long!* Sherlock can't believe his eyes. A gigantic cobra! It is green and black, pale yellow on an underbelly that is now visible as it twists. It stands up in a perfect cobra stance and looks like it wants to strike Crew. "Biggest venomous snake ever!"

Then he turns to one that Sherlock can't quite see yet, sulking, it almost seems, in a corner. Several rats and a lizard lie beside it, very still. It is nearly ten feet long, pale on its belly and purplish-black along its long top. “Mr. Holmes, look, the Inland Taipan, world’s most poisonous snake. One bite can kill one hundred people!” He glows at the boy as if his captive should be thrilled.

“Please!” cries Sherlock. “Please! Spare me!” He wishes he had not come here. He thinks of Irene and Beatrice and their tender touch. He thinks of his home above the hatter’s shop when he was a child, and of his dear friend Sigerson Bell. He wonders why he ever thought he should pursue this life of fighting crime.

“Yes?” asks Crew. He is smiling now, as if he is actually enjoying talking so much.

“I will leave here and never bother you again. I will give up crime fighting forever. I will let Malefactor be!”

“But,” whines Crew, “you have not met my greatest pet, one chosen for you, Mr. Holmes.” He turns to the wall. “Satan?” he calls out.

It emerges. It is the one Sherlock saw coiling around Crew from above, the one that looked like a monster from a book, whose size Holmes could not fully estimate. He can now. It keeps coming and coming and coming, slithering out from a place against a wall away from the others, *almost thirty feet long!* It is a sickly greenish-brown with black spots like diseases on its skin. Its head is the size of a football! Holmes can see now that it is chained to the wall near its tail, a hook impaled in it, so it cannot fully get free. Perhaps Crew fears it a little too.

“World’s largest snake!” whines the villain. “Constrictor for the ages, the ANACONDA!”

Sherlock realizes that he is seeing the thing that he had come to find tonight. *The murder weapon!* If he had only been able to live, he could have shown it to the police. He could tell them that *this* is what murdered Grimsby. They would have believed it. It is evidence enough. He thinks of that thick, purplish ring around the little man's chest, of something smashing his ribs, bursting his lungs. Something, as the doctor would testify, *inhuman.*

But it is too late now. He has miscalculated. He will never utter another word to the police.

"Come, Satan," says Crew, indicating Sherlock to the snake. He sets his pistol on the floor and bends down to unleash the reptile. In an instant, it is free! The anaconda slithers toward the bed. Holmes's eyes grow huge as he gapes at it. He begins to whimper. He cannot stop. Terror overcomes him. He thinks of his mother.

"You have much to do in life," he hears her say. When he does, he stops crying. He stiffens himself and turns on his brain. As weak as he is, he cannot give up. He looks at Crew's face, drool now coming from his lips as he anticipates seeing the anaconda crush Malefactor's greatest enemy. Crew steps forward with the snake, to get a closer look.

Don't give up.

In his fear and his feeble state, he had assumed that he had no way of fighting back. But now he thinks about Crew setting the gun down on the floor. *Why did he not retrieve it once he had loosed the snake? If I could get to my feet, he would not have a weapon.* He remembers Crew embracing him as he slammed him down onto the marble bed. *Why did he do that? He feels no affection for anyone.* He thinks of Crew caressing his arms, and it comes to him. *My horsewhip!* Crew was feeling for his horsewhip up his sleeve. *He has seen me use it before. He knows where I keep it.* But it wasn't there. *That had relaxed him. That's why he thought he could put the gun down.* It is five or ten strides behind him. Until now, he has kept his eyes glued on Sherlock. *He thinks I don't have my weapon. He is being careless, unguarded. He may even look away.* Sherlock locks his eyes onto Crew. And, just as he expects, the weird one turns away for a second, almost as if to see the expressions on his snakes' faces, as if they were a bizarre audience whose reaction to this horrible death he wants to observe.

The anaconda is within a few feet.

I must time it right.

Summoning every ounce of strength he has left, Sherlock reaches down and seizes his horsewhip, which he had put in a different place tonight, into his brand new boots that Bell had given him, that ride almost halfway up his calf. It had struck him as a much better place to conceal his great weapon.

He staggers to his feet as fast as he can, whip in hand. Both the snake and Crew, whose head has snapped back to his victim, freeze. Sherlock cracks it at the monster constrictor, wrapping it around its big head in a strangling grip. The snake writhes in pain and pulls the whip from Sherlock's hand with its fangs. Its strength is inhuman. It coils around the whip in a frenzy, squeezing itself, as though it intends to crush its own body.

"No!" cries Crew and rushes to it. His interest in Sherlock evaporates. Holmes drops from the marble bed and rushes away, dancing through the other snakes that now dart and strike at him. One bite will kill him before he even reaches London Bridge, several will make his insides explode. But he gets by the snakes, desperate not only to live, but to destroy this villain and his powerful master. In seconds he is up the steps and slamming out the door.

"Satan! My baby!" he hears Crew cry out.

It would normally take Holmes nearly half an hour to get back over the river and to Trafalgar Square just south of Denmark Street. This time, adrenaline pumping through his veins like a waterfall, he makes it in twenty minutes. But he doesn't go north there. He swings west to Scotland Yard.

His plan is still in motion.

25

TWO DOWN, ONE TO GO

It is past midnight, the early hours of the morning, black and foggy on the streets of London. Even Whitehall Street looks deserted and creepy. But Sherlock barely notices. He gets to police headquarters, stumbles up the stone steps and thunders through the thick wooden doors. His face must be as pale as a ghost's, for the night sergeant, who knows him well, looks alarmed at his appearance; and this, despite his natty attire.

"Master Holmes, what is wrong?" he cries.

"I need Lestrade!"

Young G. Lestrade is not a great detective, nor will he ever be, but he uses what brains he has to get ahead. Those brains told him long ago to make a friend of Sherlock Holmes. They also told him to be sure that Holmes has at least one other friend at Scotland Yard, in case Lestrade himself is not about when something matters. That individual is the night sergeant. This young man, not much older than G. Lestrade and low himself on the totem pole of police status, has been told in no uncertain terms – with the inducement of Lestrade's future influence to motivate him – that the brilliant half-Jew is never to be turned away if he arrives with private information for G.L.

The sergeant doesn't hesitate. "I shall send a boy!" he says and dispatches one with great haste to young Lestrade's new rooms in a lodging house in Chelsea, the first bachelor quarters of his life. The lad flies out into the night with shillings for a fast hansom cab clutched in his hand.

In less than an hour, a bleary-eyed Lestrade appears in his cramped office in Scotland Yard to see a very well-dressed but pale Sherlock Holmes moving with the energy of a hungry wolf in tight little circles on his floor.

"Holmes, what has happened?"

"Nothing. Not yet. It is about to."

"What are you saying?"

"Bring a man, a big man, a very big man, as tough as nails, and come with me. Now!"

"Come with you where and for what purpose?"

"I can prove who murdered Grimsby."

"Really?"

"I can snare him for you tonight. And when I do, I will be delivering into your hands not only a despicable villain who has already murdered countless others in his brief life, but someone who will, I guarantee, kill many more if we do not snuff him out!"

Sherlock's eyes are blazing. It almost frightens Lestrade. He often thinks that his will to fight crime is Holmes's equal, but at moments like these, he knows it is not.

"And furthermore, I believe I can, with this arrest, put before the courts someone else – the spider who spins the greatest web of crime in all of London, who plans to dominate it in future years, mastermind it, be the power behind the murder, the robbery, and the moral contamination of great masses of our populace!"

"Sherlock that is a mighty –"

"Grimsby is dead. Crew is in his lair surrounded by evidence that can destroy him. Malefactor awaits my final stroke! He will be there, tonight, I know it!"

"Calm down, my friend."

The cords are bulging in Sherlock's neck.

"Come with me! Now!"

"Where, Holmes?"

"To the Cross Bones Graveyard in Southwark!"

Lestrade is well aware of that satanic place. The very mention of it, uttered with such vehemence by the boy, makes him start. It is two o'clock in the morning, a witching hour, pitch black outside.

"Cross . . . Cross Bones?"

"Come with me, Lestrade, and make your career!"

Fifteen minutes later, Holmes, Lestrade, and the burliest constable on the night shift at Scotland Yard, a massive man named Landless with a bulldog head and three feet across the shoulders, are in a black police coach heading down Fleet Street toward London Bridge. The young detective can't believe he has been convinced to do this. Neither can he believe that he has taken the step of securing a revolver with a six-bullet chamber for this raid. But Sherlock is adamant about what awaits them. He is certain too about the reward. Nothing, he is insisting, will strike a greater blow against crime in this century than this operation tonight. Lestrade thinks of Grimsby as an inconsequential little man, Crew of only slightly greater interest, and Malefactor as a retired young street thug, now long gone from the city. But if Holmes says they are much more, they almost certainly are.

"Lestrade," says Sherlock just before they reach Southwark, "if we are to survive tonight –"

"Survive?"

"And live to be adults pursuing our noble careers, we must not be longstanding friends."

"Pardon me?"

"It is best, in the future, that we act strictly as professionals without conjoined pasts. You did not know me in my youth, nor I you. It will serve us well."

There are times when the young detective wonders if Sherlock Holmes is insane. And yet, here Lestrade is, following him into mortal danger.

When they arrive, Lestrade can barely bring himself to look at Cross Bones Graveyard, let alone enter it. The police never go near it; no one does, as far as he knows. But when he glances through the bars of the gates and sees the crypt that Holmes points out, he can't help being intrigued. He is almost convinced that he should set aside his fears. When Sherlock climbs onto the gate and leaps over, he knows he must follow. Landless boosts him up and stands behind him. He edges over the top, over the rusty spears, and drops down gingerly onto the putrid grounds. Landless follows with a thud. The giant man has the sort of thick, shaved head that has the same expression on both sides – both his face and neck are impassive, emotionless, as if they are made of hard muscle.

No one has followed them. Or is that true?

As Sherlock approaches the crypt, he motions for the other two to be silent. They are actually tiptoeing. Lestrade, unbeknownst to his companions, is fighting to keep from vomiting. The smells are overpowering him, the knowledge that he walks upon layers of rotting bodies unnerves him, and the sight of decomposing skulls unmans him. He is happy to reach the cold marble surface of the crypt and set one shaking hand against it; the other grips his revolver at the ready.

Sherlock is sure that Crew will still be in the crypt. The villain fears no man – he will not care that Holmes knows where he lives. Nor does he have any idea that Sherlock has the evidence to convict him of Grimsby's murder.

The boy has a plan. Now he just needs to execute it.

When they reach the hole in the wall, Lestrade is instructed to peer in. He does so for a long time and when he finally pulls his face back, the startled look in his eyes indicates that Crew is back on his marble bed with his extraordinary snakes. Sherlock takes a glance too. Satan looks to have survived his desperate grapple with the horsewhip, his deathly attack upon himself, and Crew is virtually purring as he lies amongst his colorful reptilian charges.

It is time to move in.

Holmes whispers into Lestrade's ear and then sneaks around to the door of the crypt. He finds the keyhole and begins working on the lock inside it. He has sprung similar puzzlers over the years, his skill borne of instructions he's secretly heard Malefactor give his minions. He even keeps a tool for these purposes now, a perfectly pointed and bent big pin.

But it doesn't work tonight.

As he labors away, the door suddenly opens with great violence, knocking him forcefully to the ground. His face is driven into the smelly earth and Crew again has him by the neck.

"Sherlock Holmes," whines Crew, right into his ear as he lies on top of him, "being stupid." He hauls him to the door, closes it behind them, and drags him down the stairs again, muttering. "Sherlock Holmes almost killed Satan. Sherlock Holmes must die." He slams him onto the marble bed again. He has no need to feel the boy's arms or even inspect his boots this time. The boy carries no weapons in his hands, and the horsewhip lies in the swamp water, where Satan now keeps it.

"Jew-boy will die. Hate Jews. Hate," says Crew. As he turns, he keeps whispering, "Hate darkies, hate Chinamen. Hate." This time he doesn't bother to call on the Black Mamba, the Taipan, the Sidewinder, or the Saw-Scaled Viper – he merely asks for the giant anaconda. It is no longer tethered.

"Satan?" he says, as though inquiring if a child would like a candy. The big reptile crawls forward.

"Is this what you did to the others?" asks Sherlock in a shaking voice.

"Not them all."

"But some?"

"Oh, yes. Great fun."

"Who?"

Satan is out of his swamp, slithering across the floor. He is between Crew and Sherlock. The boy is weaponless and cannot get away.

The fiend names a few men, mostly well-known criminals who stood in Malefactor's way, who have disappeared from the streets the last few years. Crew lists his victims with great pride, uttering each name clearly.

"I knew it," says Holmes.

"Clever Jew."

"You did it for Malefactor."

"Malefactor, yes. Not his real name." Crew almost bows, and shakes his head.

"And Grimsby?" Sherlock's eyes are large, staring at the anaconda.

"Grimsby?" asks Crew.

Satan is nearly at the bed.

"He was thrown into the river near here!" cries Holmes. "He had a horrible, thick welt around his chest! His ribs were broken! He was squeezed to death, the doctor said, the doctor will testify, by something inhuman!"

The anaconda is getting closer. The boy appears

absolutely terrified. Crew would never dream of letting him go now. He *has* him. He isn't even bothering to use his derringer pistol.

Up at the hole in the wall outside in the graveyard, Lestrade is watching and listening and astonished. Holmes has figured it out! There is no one like him. He is destined for greatness, Lestrade is certain.

Landless has his ear near the young detective, listening too, a second witness.

"Clever theory, clever plan," says Crew again. "Clever Jew must die."

Satan reaches the bed and slides onto it, showing his fangs as he touches Sherlock's boots.

Lestrade is running now, Landless at his side, leaving at just the moment they were instructed to make their move. They rush for the locked door.

But inside, Satan is already halfway up Sherlock's trousers, slipping his huge head between his legs, beginning to coil around him. The boy cries out.

Lestrade and Landless reach the door. The detective fires at the keyhole, just as he was told to do, and blows it to smithereens.

But now Satan has begun to pull Sherlock Holmes into an inhuman hug. He is wrapping around him, climbing up his torso. It won't take long.

Crew's head had shot up at the gun blast. As he turns now to the stairs, he sees Lestrade and a gigantic policeman with a head like a bulldog's, flying downward. "Holmes? Not stupid," he whines. "I should have . . ."

Satan is beginning to squeeze. Sherlock has never felt anything like it. He is wrapped in a warm embrace. At first, it is strangely kind, almost loving. Holmes doesn't know whether to resist or let it happen. *Which would give me an extra second?* Instantly, he cannot breathe. He shrieks.

"LESTRADE!"

The big anaconda has raised its head to see what is happening on the stairs. The young detective cocks the gun.

"No!" screams Crew.

Lestrade fires. Satan's head explodes.

"Clever Jew," cries Crew, beginning to sob.

The anaconda's coil springs loose like a jack-in-the-box releasing. Sherlock writhes out of it as if he were in excrement, kicking at the monster that had held him tightly, catching his breath. Lestrade points the gun toward the other snakes, his eyes wide, his hands shaking, training it on one and then another. They move toward him, hissing, standing up on ends, fangs bared.

"No shooting!" shouts Crew. He says something incomprehensible to his snakes, as if speaking in an evil tongue, and they back away, slithering to the walls, the plants, and into the swamp water.

Landless takes three giant strides across the room and seizes Crew.

But out of the blue, another voice echoes in the room. "No one move!" it snarls.

They all freeze.

A man in a tailcoat and top hat, with sunken eyes, a tongue darting along his thin lips like a lizard, and a bulging forehead, is stepping slowly down the stairs and into the crypt. He has a walking stick in hand. He pulls on it and produces an air gun from its insides. He has entered at precisely the moment that Lestrade turned to Crew, putting his back to the entrance. The man trains his gun on the rear of the young detective's skull.

Malefactor.

26

CONFRONTATION

It is what Holmes was hoping for – he had known that Malefactor was out there watching him, had been on his trail these last few days even though he had done so like a shadow, more invisible than he had ever been before. Sherlock had also known that Malefactor had wanted to stay out of things, simply let Crew destroy his rival for him. But Holmes knew that if he could put Crew into this situation and corner him, Malefactor would show himself.

"This is your man!" cries Sherlock to Lestrade, pointing at his great opponent.

"I prefer 'professor.' You are well dressed tonight, Holmes! My compliments to you."

"Observe him!"

"Drop your weapon," says Malefactor to Lestrade. "You and your brainless giant and the meddling half-Jew will not lay a hand upon Mr. Crew. Your time on this earth, your time obstructing my plans, is over."

"No," says Holmes to Lestrade, "don't move."

The young detective looks terrified. He seems about to soil his trousers. He maintains his grip on his revolver as much out of fear as decision.

Holmes leaps from the bed and runs. He rushes past a startled Malefactor and is almost up the stairs before his enemy can consider firing. Lestrade and Landless dart behind Crew.

Malefactor must make a decision. He must tend to them or chase me. If he even takes the time to try to wound them, I will be lost. I know which one he will choose.

Sherlock is barely into the graveyard when he hears running footsteps behind him.

The villain has sacrificed Crew. Grimsby is dead. There are two down and one to go, the big one.

Holmes takes him on a race up Redcross Street, through St. Saviour's Cemetery, and back across London Bridge. Just before they left Scotland Yard, he had told Lestrade to muster a half dozen Bobbies, arm them all, and send them to Cross Bones when they were ready. He is calculating that the Force will be coming up Fleet Street now or on Cannon Street or nearing it, about to turn toward London Bridge. *They will seize anyone who is chasing me, especially if he is bearing a weapon.*

Sherlock is thrilled. Even as he runs, even as he worries that Malefactor may be able to hit him with one good shot from behind, he is filled with an overwhelming sense of anticipation. He has caught the other two, and now he will snare the biggest fish of all, the one with whom he has been battling for so many years. He is guessing that even if Malefactor can find a moment to fire accurately, he will prefer to wing him, perhaps injure him in a leg, so he can approach him, haul him down to the river, and finish him there, looking into his eyes. But the monster does not know that Holmes has everything planned. The Bobbies will soon be here.

But it is isn't the Force that the boy sees as he reaches the top of the stone stairs that descend from the bridge down to the street on the north side of the river. He stops. Malefactor is more than halfway over the viaduct behind him, close enough to spot him clearly and take an accurate shot.

It is Sigerson Bell.

The old man is coming their way, somehow marching at a good clip, using every ounce of energy he has left in his body. His face looks milk white, his eyes, even from here and behind his spectacles, are fire red, almost shining in the night. He is coughing horribly. Everything about his sickly form and struggling movements shouts determination. He is dressed in his best black suit, the one he once told Sherlock his mother gave him to wear at his own funeral. Sherlock knows that the old man is coming to see him to say good-bye.

"RUN!!!" cries the boy.

But when Bell runs, he runs the wrong way. Instead of turning around and making for Cannon Street or Cheapside, in the direction from which the police will be coming, he heads east along Lower Thames Street toward the Tower of London. Thankful that Malefactor hasn't fired, Sherlock flies down the steps and tears after the old man, calling out, telling him to turn the other way. But the ancient apothecary, running in a stagger, keeps moving, aware that his charge is frightened, that he is in danger, and that he must take to his heels and get away as best he can.

"AH!" cries Malefactor when he reaches the top of the stairs. He fires a shot. It isn't directed at Holmes. He shoots at Sigerson Bell.

Sherlock is beside himself with terror. The villain is trying to kill his dear friend, knowing instinctively that this will be to his advantage; it will either bring Holmes to a halt or slow him down if he needs to help his old mentor run, if he must carry him.

The boy's plans are in tatters. Now that he is chasing after Bell in the wrong direction, *all* is lost. Malefactor will soon be at the bottom of the stairs and then running after them. In minutes, the police will have passed them, gone up the stairs and over the bridge toward Cross Bones. Every chance to not just collar him, but perhaps save themselves, will be lost.

Sherlock has no choice now. He must try to rescue Bell and himself. But that seems impossible. In less than a minute, he has caught up to the old apothecary. He doesn't say a word to him, doesn't reproach him for making the wrong decision. *How could he have known?* Sherlock berates himself for not telling Bell everything. It had seemed that he was giving him *so* much information over the past few days, *too* much information – that was by design – but really, he wasn't telling him what mattered: his great secret. Now, it is too late. They simply have to survive.

He takes Bell by the arm and helps him run. They are at the Billingsgate Fish Market, where he had forced Malefactor to help him with the Whitechapel murder long ago. It seems like ages since they met here. The smell of fish and the odors of the river fill the dark air. There are few gaslamps in the area. The Tower of London looms ahead, beyond it St. Katherine's Dock, and then the massive Docks of London.

But, slowed by the old man's infirmities, they don't get past the Tower. Malefactor gains on them quickly. When they come to the far side of the Tower Wharf, about to reach St. Katherine's Dock, he fires a shot that goes between their heads. Sherlock knows it is time to surrender. Perhaps he can save his friend. He stops running, releases Bell, and pushes him away. They are just where the wharf rises highest above the river. A big ship, a fancy new steamer, sits in the water nearby, being repaired, a crane over it with pulleys hanging down.

Curiously, Bell doesn't object to being shoved away from Holmes. In fact, he shuffles right to the very edge of the high wharf as Sherlock steps toward his mortal enemy.

"Kill me," he says. "Let the old man be. He is dying. Give him his last hours."

Malefactor looks from one target to the other. His lizard tongue darts out and licks his lips. His sunken eyes shine, his bulging white head glows in the night. There had been a time when Sherlock had thought this villain to be a sort of romantic figure, a rogue of the night. Irene had thought that too, for a while. She had been drawn to this bad boy. But she knows better now, and so does Sherlock Holmes. There is nothing attractive about Malefactor, or whatever his name is. There is nothing attractive about evil. The street thug is still a street thug, professor or not, refined language or not. It seems to Sherlock that as this fiend's depravity has grown, his looks have diminished. An ugly man now stands before them with ugly intentions.

"I shall be glad to finish you, Holmes. In fact, I will do it without my weapon. You and I shall wrestle here on the banks of the River Thames to see who is the better man. You may think that you are equipped to defeat me with your skills, but you will be surprised."

"Very surprised," says Sigerson Bell.

Malefactor looks irritated. "He would do best to close his mouth."

"Mr. Bell," pleads Sherlock, "please, let *me* confront him."

"Were I healthy," continues Bell, ignoring his apprentice, "I would defeat you myself. You are a coward and a thief. You pretend that the hardships of your youth, which were your criminal family's own fault, give you the right to be a selfish pig and hurt others."

"Old man," says Malefactor, "be quiet!"

"I doubt it is you who kills your victims anyway. I assume you have that animal, Crew, do all your dirty work."

"Would you like to see some of my *dirty work*, old man?"

"Mr. Bell, please, be quiet!" says Sherlock.

Malefactor steps toward Bell, still training his air gun on Sherlock.

"No, please, don't," says Holmes.

The young crime boss picks up momentum as he advances in Bell's direction. The apothecary now looks as if he were about to faint; he staggers on the very edge of the wharf, reeling there, the water a great distance below, the ship with the hanging pulleys just a few feet away.

With a smile, Malefactor takes a mighty swing at the old man, to drive the gun into his face and knock him unconscious into the river.

But Sigerson Bell has been faking. The instant Malefactor swings at him, throwing himself forward, the apothecary pulls his head away like lightning. When the villain misses, he goes completely off balance, teeters on the edge, and falls. As he drops, his head strikes a big iron pulley. When he enters the water with a splash, he is limp.

27

MASTER SHERLOCK

Sherlock runs to the edge and takes Bell into his arms and keeps him from falling as they both look down into the water. Malefactor has disappeared in the river. Big concentric circles form on the surface. He doesn't come back up.

They stand there for several minutes, saying nothing, the sounds of London in the background – horses and carriages and fading shouts in the distance, foghorns nearer on the river.

"My boy," says Sigerson Bell weakly, now looking as if he might collapse, "I want to go up to the bridge. There are things I must ask you and other things I must tell you."

"Why are you wearing this suit, sir?"

"Never mind."

It takes them a while to get up to the bridge. No longer motivated to find or save his apprentice, Bell is so feeble that he can barely walk. It is amazing that he even summoned the energy to come to this area tonight, and incredible that he had it in him to confront Malefactor. It was as if some unseen force, given to him by God or the gods, empowered him when he needed it, when he had to help Sherlock Holmes.

They stand in the middle of the bridge, far above the black water, leaning on the thick stone balustrade, dim gas lamps above them. The Tower of London, white and light brown during the day, gray and black at night, looms to their left down by the banks, the rest of the great city behind them. Sherlock can still see the ship docked where Malefactor met his fate.

"I am about to die," says Bell.

"No!"

"Yes, I am. And that is not a bad thing. Everyone's life comes to an end, though I shall miss you." Sherlock detects tears welling in the old man's eyes, but he shakes his head, as if to send them away. "The Esquimaux who live in the arctic regions of the newly formed country of Canada have a tradition, I hear, when they grow aged and useless. They merely walk out into the snow and die. I like that. It seems very brave and practical, not to mention poetic. I should like to do something like that."

"I should prefer that you live, sir." Sherlock is finding it hard not to break down. He got all that he wanted tonight, but to lose Sigerson Bell would make everything for naught.

"I should not. I believe in the rhythms of life. I am descended from the Trismegistus family, as I have often said. The first Trismegistus, the great one, was a man who, legend says, in ancient times, made himself into a god. He wasn't *the* God, mind, but *a* god. He believed that human beings could be so much more than they are. Alchemy is like that too. It theorizes that materials can be turned into gold. I have always held to that principle. I have held to it in my education of one Sherlock Holmes."

The boy smiles.

"You, sir," says Bell, "were like a gift to me. And you can be a gift to humankind. You believe in the right things. I shall leave you to it. I shall leave you to being the sword of justice that this city, this country, this world needs. I believe in you. I believe you are destined for greatness. It need not be anything that you broadcast to the world, though I imagine you will, since you have a sprightly sense of yourself, my boy, which powers you at times. You will find a way, a person, perhaps, to tell everyone how great you are."

"Sir, I doubt I will . . ."

Bell smiles. "That is fine." His face darkens. "But there is something else that is not fine, not fine about you."

Sherlock is taken aback. "What have I done, sir?"

"You have been keeping a secret from me, this last week or so."

Sherlock swallows. "A secret?"

"And now, you are about to tell me that secret. It is important that you do so before I die."

"I don't know what you are –"

"Who killed Grimsby, Sherlock?"

"Well, I will prove that it was Crew."

"Yes, you will, but who *really* killed him? Who murdered Grimsby?"

"I don't know what you –"

"I taught you some deadly Bellitsu, Sherlock, did I not? I remember a particularly 'inhuman' maneuver."

"I –"

"Who murdered Grimsby?"

"Uh . . ."

"Say his name. Tell me, my boy, who murdered Grimsby in cold blood?" Bell looks angry. "Say the name of the villain who murdered him!"

The boy hesitates and then lowers his head.

"Sherlock Holmes," he says. "I *killed* him. I murdered that swine, down here near the docks!"

"Yes, you did. With a Bellitsu move, a bear hug administered in just the right place to crush four ribs, puncture the lungs, and squeeze the life out of that little man. I taught you to do something so brutal, so decisive that even a doctor wouldn't believe a human being had done it."

"Grimsby was evil. He deserved it."

"The first part is correct. The rest is for the courts and for God to decide, not you."

"I was angry."

"I know."

"My mother . . ." Sherlock holds back tears. Bell puts his arm around him. "And then that poor little girl with the monster head with nothing in life but her kind blue eyes. My mother had blue eyes. I wanted to kill him the moment he took her life. I had had enough. I knew that he and Crew and Malefactor would be the instruments of the murder of many more if they were allowed to go on. I didn't know how to stop him. The woman in Hounslow said I couldn't tell anyone. He was going to get away with it again. He was going to ascend in the Treasury and contaminate our city and our country, our world. There are so few people who do evil, but they destroy life for so many. I went out that night. I tracked him like a hound. I knew the part of the city he would be in. I knew he would be frightened of Malefactor, not wanting to go home. I was sure he would be running in the streets he knew. So I went there. I found him. I destroyed him."

"And, after you did it, you saw an opportunity, didn't you?"

"Yes. Irene said I should seek his killer and so did you."

"A fine idea, a just one."

"Yes, you are right. But that killer was me. And when Malefactor came to see me in that public house in Leicester Square, he was SO angry; he hated Grimsby for his interference. It came to me suddenly that I could frame him. I could frame them all. I had killed Grimsby, Crew could be positioned as his murderer to the police, and Malefactor, filled with hate for his disloyal lieutenant and with a motive to kill him, could be shown to be the power behind it all."

"You just needed a plan."

"It came quickly. I began telling you and my brother Mycroft and every one I met that I was seeking the murderer of one Grimsby. I even made Lestrade note it in the police records. The seeker of the murderer is never the murderer himself. I wanted everyone, from the police on down, to think me the least possible suspect. That is what criminals should do."

"Then you went after Crew. You found out about the snakes that he carried. You searched for his home, the lair no one else dared near. Snakes! It was perfect! You have seen them, haven't you? Was one a big constrictor, capable of killing a large mammal?"

"Yes, sir, an anaconda."

"An anaconda's squeeze! That would be 'inhuman,' that would leave a huge purple welt across the chest of the victim and crush his insides. The police would believe that."

"Yes, they will."

"Despite the fact that the anaconda would have left a series of welts, not just one, as you did."

"Lestrade won't figure that out."

"He won't know much about an exotic snake from the Amazon, will he? He won't know that it might have tried to swallow its victim too, especially a little one like Grimsby."

The boy pauses. "Should I tell him everything?"

"No, Sherlock, you shouldn't."

"No?"

"Though I am not glad that you took Grimsby's life, I am glad that he is dead. Good riddance to him! I am also glad that Crew will be hanged for his murder and for the murder of many others. Good riddance to him too! Malefactor, thank goodness, is gone, though I don't believe he would have been convicted on the evidence you provided. Had he lived, I have no doubt, given his genius, he would have walked free."

"I . . . I am sorry, sir. I was too angry. I wanted to stop them so much!" He begins to cry. Bell embraces him. They have never done anything quite like this before.

"You are forgiven, my boy. Now, go out and *never* do such a thing again. Respect yourself and respect others. Always do what is right, no matter what, no matter your opponent, no matter their evil. Oh, be tricky, my young knight, use means that are irregular, even a little nasty, shall we say, and always win! Be your brilliant self. You *must* win! But never do the evil that they do."

"I won't."

"The world needs you. You have much to do in life."

When he utters those words, the same words that Sherlock's mother said to him before she died, the boy looks at Bell. *Did I ever tell him that?* A shiver goes through him. Who is this man, really? *Was he sent to me?* Bell pulls back from him and smiles. Then, the old man struggles up onto the balustrade, teetering over the water far below. Sherlock doesn't stop him.

"I shall bequeath the entire shop to you, my boy. Sell it. Keep the money and go to university. Go to the best, to Oxford or Cambridge. You will need connections to get there, despite your genius. That's how it works in our world. Go to see Sir Ramsay Stonefield. He will be overjoyed at what you have done for him. I am sure you can ask Lestrade to keep his good name out of all of this. In a year or two, with Stonefield's influence, you will be in any school of your choosing."

Bell looks down at the water and spreads out his arms.

"We all came from water, my boy. We should all return there."

And with that, he lets himself fall from the bridge. Sherlock gasps, but he doesn't run to the edge and look over.

He hears the splash. It sounds so tiny for such a gigantic man.

So, it ends.

Sherlock walks away. The police will soon be coming over the bridge from Southwark with Crew in chains. Holmes doesn't want to see them. He simply wants to go home to the apothecary shop. He will not cry. He will not think of Bell or Irene or Beatrice or his mother or father. For their sake, for the sake of many others, he will not break down. From this day forward, he will not think anymore of his entire childhood. He knows now that emotions are his enemy. He must be a machine, a sword against evil. *My past shall be known to no one. I will be a mystery, my vulnerabilities unavailable to the criminals.* He will sell the shop, speak to Stonefield, go to university, come back to London, to the center of both good and evil, and set himself up here. He will fight crime in a manner and with a success that no one else has ever achieved. And, yes, he will find someone to tell the world about it.

It occurs to him that he has a home again. His home, his solace in life, is in his great purpose.

At least, he thinks, *I have a head start. I have vanquished Malefactor.*

He leans over the balustrade for a moment, just before he descends the stairs back into the city. The sun is beginning to rise. From where he is, he can see the Tower of London better than before. Its wharf is clear, right in front of that ship where Malefactor went under. As he looks down there, he sees something.

A man is lying on the wharf right near the ship. He is soaking wet, having just pulled himself from the water. He is dressed in black, wearing a tailcoat. He staggers to his feet, holding his head. For an instant, he seems to steal a glance over his shoulder up toward London Bridge where Sherlock stands.

The villain walks away.

The young man up on the bridge isn't disappointed. He is ready. *I am a man.* A smile comes to his lips. He feels as strong as the anaconda. Much stronger, in fact.

It is dawn, thinks Sherlock Holmes. *It is just the beginning.*

Be sure to read the first five books in the award-winning series

EYE OF THE CROW

It is the spring of 1867, and a yellow fog hangs over London. In the dead of night, a woman is brutally stabbed and left to die in a pool of blood. No one sees the terrible crime. Or so it seems.

Nearby, a brilliant, bitter boy dreams of a better life. He is the son of a Jewish intellectual and a highborn lady – social outcasts – impoverishment the price of their mixed marriage. The boy's name is Sherlock Holmes.

Strangely compelled to visit the scene, Sherlock comes face to face with the young Arab wrongly accused of the crime. By degrees, he is drawn to the center of the mystery, until he, too, is a suspect.

Danger runs high in this desperate quest for justice. As the clues mount, Sherlock sees the murder through the eye of its only witness. But a fatal mistake and its shocking consequence change everything and put him squarely on a path to becoming a complex man with a dark past – and the world's greatest detective.

DEATH IN THE AIR

Still reeling from his mother's death, brought about by his involvement in solving London's brutal East End murder, young Sherlock Holmes commits himself to fighting crime . . . and is soon immersed in another case.

While visiting his father at work, Sherlock stops to watch a dangerous high-trapeze performance, framed by the magnificent glass ceiling of the legendary Crystal Palace. But without warning, the aerialist drops, screaming and flailing to the floor. He lands with a sickening thud, just feet away and rolls almost onto the boy's boots. He is bleeding profusely and his body is grotesquely twisted. Leaning over, Sherlock brings his ear up close. "Silence me . . ." the man gasps and then lies still. In the mayhem that follows, the boy notices something amiss that no one else sees – and he knows that foul play is afoot. What he doesn't know is that his discovery will set him on a trail that leads to an entire gang of notorious and utterly ruthless criminals.

VANISHING GIRL

When a wealthy young socialite mysteriously vanishes in Hyde Park, young Sherlock Holmes is compelled to prove himself once more. There is much at stake: the kidnap victim, an innocent child's survival, the fragile relationship between himself and the beautiful Irene Doyle. Sherlock must act quickly if he is to avoid the growing menace of his enemy, Malefactor, and further humiliation at the hands of Scotland Yard.

As twisted and dangerous as the backstreets of Victorian London, this third case in The Boy Sherlock Holmes series takes the youth on a heart-stopping race against time to the countryside, the coast, and into the haunted lair of exotic – and deadly – night creatures.

Despite the cold, the loneliness, the danger, and the memories of his shattered family, one thought keeps Sherlock going; soon, very soon, the world will come to know him as the master detective of all time.

DEATH IN THE AIR

Still reeling from his mother's death, brought about by his involvement in solving London's brutal East End murder, young Sherlock Holmes commits himself to fighting crime . . . and is soon immersed in another case.

While visiting his father at work, Sherlock stops to watch a dangerous high-trapeze performance, framed by the magnificent glass ceiling of the legendary Crystal Palace. But without warning, the aerialist drops, screaming and flailing to the floor. He lands with a sickening thud, just feet away and rolls almost onto the boy's boots. He is bleeding profusely and his body is grotesquely twisted. Leaning over, Sherlock brings his ear up close. "Silence me . . ." the man gasps and then lies still. In the mayhem that follows, the boy notices something amiss that no one else sees – and he knows that foul play is afoot. What he doesn't know is that his discovery will set him on a trail that leads to an entire gang of notorious and utterly ruthless criminals.

VANISHING GIRL

When a wealthy young socialite mysteriously vanishes in Hyde Park, young Sherlock Holmes is compelled to prove himself once more. There is much at stake: the kidnap victim, an innocent child's survival, the fragile relationship between himself and the beautiful Irene Doyle. Sherlock must act quickly if he is to avoid the growing menace of his enemy, Malefactor, and further humiliation at the hands of Scotland Yard.

As twisted and dangerous as the backstreets of Victorian London, this third case in The Boy Sherlock Holmes series takes the youth on a heart-stopping race against time to the countryside, the coast, and into the haunted lair of exotic – and deadly – night creatures.

Despite the cold, the loneliness, the danger, and the memories of his shattered family, one thought keeps Sherlock going; soon, very soon, the world will come to know him as the master detective of all time.

THE SECRET FIEND

In 1868, Benjamin Disraeli becomes England's first Jewish-born prime minister. Sherlock Holmes welcomes the event – but others fear it. The upper classes worry that the black-haired Hebrew cannot be good for the empire. The wealthy hear rumblings as the poor hunger for sweeping improvements to their lot in life. The winds of change are blowing.

Late one night, Sherlock's admirer and former schoolmate, Beatrice, arrives at his door, terrified. She claims a maniacal, bat-like man has leapt upon her and her friend on Westminster Bridge. The fiend she describes is the Spring Heeled Jack, a fictional character from the old Penny Dreadful thrillers. Moreover, Beatrice declares the Jack has made off with her friend. She begs Holmes to help, but he finds the story incredible. Reluctant to return to detective work, he pays little heed – until the attacks increase, and Spring Heeled Jacks seem to be everywhere. Now, all of London has more to worry about than politics. Before he knows it, the unwilling boy detective is thrust, once more, into the heart of a deadly mystery, in which everyone, even his closest friend and mentor, is suspect.

THE DRAGON TURN

Sherlock Holmes and Irene Doyle are as riveted as the rest of the audience. They are celebrating Irene's sixteenth birthday at The Egyptian Hall as Alistair Hemsworth produces a real and very deadly dragon before their eyes. This single, fantastic illusion elevates the previously unheralded magician to star status, making him the talk of London. He even outshines the Wizard of Nottingham, his rival on and off the stage.

Sherlock and Irene rush backstage after the show to meet the great man, only to witness Inspector Lestrade and his son arrest the performer. It seems one-upmanship has not been as satisfying to Hemsworth as the notion of murder. The Wizard is missing; his spectacles and chunks of flesh have been discovered in pools of blood in Hemsworth's secret workshop. That, plus the fact that Nottingham has stolen Hemsworth's wife away, speak of foul play *and* motive. There is no body, but there has certainly been a grisly death.

In this spine-tingling case, lust for fame and thirst for blood draw Sherlock Holmes one giant step closer to his destiny – master detective of all time.